After Effects

By the Same Author

The Religious Body
A Most Contagious Game
Henrietta Who?
The Complete Steel
A Late Phoenix
His Burial Too
Slight Mourning
Parting Breath
Some Die Eloquent
Passing Strange
Last Respects
Harm's Way
A Dead Liberty
The Body Politic
A Going Concern
Injury Time (short stories)

Catherine Aird

After Effects

St. Martin's Press ≈ New York

M
aird

Extracts from *The Doctor's Dilemma* by Bernard Shaw
reproduced by kind permission of The Society of Authors
on behalf of the Bernard Shaw estate.

Library of Congress Cataloging-in-Publication Data

Aird, Catherine
After effects : a Detective Inspector C.D. Sloan mystery /
Catherine Aird.
p.   cm.
ISBN 0-312-14270-6
1. Sloan, C.D. (Fictitious character)—Fiction.
2. Police—England—Fiction.   I. Title.
PR6051.I65A68   1996
823'.914—dc20   96-3514   CIP

First published in Great Britain by Macmillan,
an imprint of Macmillan General Books

First U.S. Edition: August 1996

10   9   8   7   6   5   4   3   2   1

The chapter headings are taken from
The Doctor's Dilemma – A Tragedy
by Bernard Shaw (1913).

for Margaret, Elizabeth, Sarah
and Nicholas with love

Chapter One

The patient was a hardy old lady who was not easily killed.

'St Ninian's Hospital,' said the girl on the switchboard. 'Dr Beaumont? Hold the line, please . . . putting you through . . . St Ninian's Hospital . . . Forman Ward? . . . It's ringing now . . . St Ninian's Hospital . . . I'm afraid there's no reply from Psychiatric Appointments, caller. Will you hold?'

What the caller said in answer to this simple question brought an affronted flush to the telephone operator's cheek but she had been well trained and merely offered, in impersonal, detached tones, to try the number again if the caller wished.

'St Ninian's Hospital . . .' The switchboard operator, whose name was Shirley Partridge, had developed a special sing-song voice quite unlike her everyday speech – which was pure Calleshire – for using at work. This, like the old-fashioned cubicle in which she worked, served to separate

1

her from the real world in more senses than one.

'St Ninian's Hospital . . .' She gave her response to the next caller with the same sure promptness as a programmed robot. 'Barnesdale Ward? I'm afraid the number's engaged. Will you hold or try later?'

Shirley Partridge glanced at the clock and wondered if it was too early to unscrew her thermos flask of coffee. 'St Ninian's Hospital . . . Mr McGrew's Clinic Secretary? Ringing now . . . Mr Maldonson? He's not in yet, I'm afraid, Sister.'

The telephonist knew that Mr Maldonson, the Senior Consultant Obstetrician and Gynaecologist, wasn't in the hospital because his Registrar, Dr Marion Teal, had asked her this twice already this morning.

'St Ninian's Hospital . . . Dr Byville? No. He said to say if he wasn't at Berebury he'd be over at the Safety of Drugs Committee at Calleford all morning.' Shirley Partridge prided herself on keeping tabs on the whereabouts of all the hospital's medical staff. You never knew when they'd be wanted in a hurry.

'Switchboard.' This was Shirley's usual response to a call coming up on an inside line, the internal telephone system at the old hospital not yet being fully automated. 'Dr Meggie? No, he hasn't arrived yet.' She shifted her head a fraction so that she could see the wooden 'In and Out' attendance board better. The line with the name of Dr P. E. L. Meggie, Con-

sultant Physician, on it was clearly showing 'Out'
still, in spite of the fact that it had already gone ten
o'clock in the morning on a busy Friday.

As Shirley Partridge knew very well, Dr Paul
Meggie, the hospital's senior physician, always had
a clinic on Friday mornings. She also knew very well
– but did not say so to the unknown caller – that
Martin Friar, Dr Meggie's unfortunate Senior Registrar, had been rung up quite early this morning and
detailed to start that clinic on Dr Meggie's behalf.

She knew, too, that this would occasion mixed
feelings in the registrar – torn, as he was, between
serious overwork and the desire for greater experience. She was also aware that the patients who had
come to see the great man himself at his clinic would
be unhappy about seeing his registrar instead. She
took both facts in her stride, neither being her problem. Shirley Partridge had never been one for taking
on other people's problems.

Both parties had her sympathy.

The Senior Registrar had looked tired out before
he had even started work this morning; and the
clinic patients naturally weren't going to like being
fobbed off by being seen by someone medically
speaking – they thought, anyway – still wet behind
the ears. And for another thing they weren't going to
like the way he dressed any more than Shirley did.

'Informally,' was how she had described it to her
mother. 'Not even a jacket . . .'

3

Now their Dr Paul Meggie was quite different. He always wore a dark pin-stripe suit under his spotless white coat. And he was never seen at the hospital in the mornings without his bow-tie and floral button-hole. 'A fresh one every day,' Shirley reported again and again to her mother. This week it had been the tiniest of yellow carnations.

Late for his clinic or not, as far as Shirley Partridge was concerned, Dr Paul Meggie was a Great Man and in her considered opinion the patients were lucky even to catch a quick glimpse of him. That alone – just setting eyes on him – did some of the people who were ill a lot of good. They said upstairs at the hospital that he'd only got to step on to the ward for the atmosphere to change at once.

Electrify, some of the nurses said.

'St Ninian's Hospital ... Accident and Emergency ... of course, right away.' They always answered quickly at that unit, which was something. 'St Ninian's Hospital ... Lorkyn Ward ... putting you through.' For some long-forgotten antiquarian reason the wards at St Ninian's Hospital had been named after noted medical practitioners of the sixteenth century. 'Ringing now,' sang Shirley in her working voice.

There was nothing in any way electrifying about the way in which Dr Martin Friar entered the Medical

Out-Patients' Clinic that morning. Dr Meggie's Senior Registrar was so tired that for two pins – or, better still, an unbroken night's sleep – he would have given up the profession of medicine altogether there and then. He moved into the consulting room at the clinic now with the slow measured step of one consciously conserving his reserves of energy.

'Big clinic today, Sister?' he asked.

'Not particularly,' she said kindly, bending the truth a little, and knowing that he would be feeling better after coffee-time.

'Anything interesting?'

'One or two of the new cases perhaps.' She placed the virgin folder that indicated a fresh patient in front of him. The sight of thin, unsullied hospital medical records always cheered the young doctors, just as a pile of thick, fat ones awaiting them on the desk sent a sigh of despair through whoever was taking the clinic. The thick folders usually belonged to those who were called 'heart-sink' patients, for the very good reason that they caused just that very sensation in the breasts of their weary doctors. Thin folders at least offered the chance of making an interesting diagnosis . . .

The Senior Registrar picked up the blank record of a new patient. 'Mrs Mabel Allison of Great Rooden? That's right out in the country, isn't it? All right, Sister, just give me half a minute to read the GP's referral letter and then you can call her in.'

At the same time Shirley Partridge was answering a call on her switchboard in yet another way.

'Morning, Tracy,' she said, there being no need to enquire who would be on the end of this particular line. It was a direct land-line connection between St Ninian's Hospital, which was on the coast at Kinnisport, and the Berebury District General Hospital over in Berebury, the market town in the centre of rural Calleshire.

The hospital at Berebury was a spanking new one with state-of-the-art equipment and all that medical technology could dream up in the name of progress. St Ninian's, on the other hand, was an old Poor Law institution: not to put too fine a point on it, it had been a workhouse before the advent of the National Health Service. True, it had been upgraded as far as was humanly possible – even now there was an artist labouring away on the painting of a colourful mural in the main entrance hall – but there was still that about the old raw brick building which betokened a more rugged past.

'That you, Shirl?' asked the voice at the other end of the land-line.

The two hospitals were run in tandem under one unified health authority. They shared consultant staff – which was no problem – and some facilities – which was the cause of a lot of rancour. In theory and at a pinch when beds were short – they would house each other's patients but it didn't happen often.

And never without some delicate horse-trading over waiting lists.

'Listen, Shirl,' said Tracy, who, as Shirley regularly complained to her mother, had no proper respect for her elders. 'You got Dr Beaumont over there?'

Shirley Partridge didn't need to look up at the staff attendance board to answer her. Dr Edwin Beaumont was always on time. He was in, all right. She herself had seen him step delicately round the painter who was working on the wall of the entrance lobby when Dr Beaumont had come in.

Not painter, she reminded herself.

Artist.

'Good,' said Tracy swiftly. 'Then can you put me through to him p.d.q.? Female Medical are carrying on like there's no today let alone no tomorrow—'

The wards at the new Berebury General Hospital didn't enjoy names redolent of an historic medical past. They were known by what went on in them and that, even the post-modernists were prepared to admit, did lead to some embarrassing moments.

'—and Sister Pocock's going spare,' went on Tracy, 'because she can't get hold of anyone.'

'Right away.' Actually, Shirley had been all ready to complain to Tracy about how the smell of paint in the hall was upsetting her delicate digestion –

7

stomach was not a word used in the Partridge ménage – but that would have to wait.

Tracy drew breath and went on, 'Sounds like there's open warfare up there on Female Medical. You know what Sister Pocock's like.'

'You're through.' Shirley Partridge, much as she disapproved of Tracy's free and easy way of putting things, hooked in the telephone connection without delay.

'Ta, ever so ta.' Young Tracy usually used what spare time she had on the land-line talking to Shirley about her current boyfriend and what she'd been up to the night before – well, nearly everything – but this was not the moment for that.

'Dr Beaumont'll soon sort it out,' said Shirley confidently as the telephone connection was made. She liked him. Dr Beaumont dressed properly and was always polite to switchboard operators, too. 'Whatever it is.'

'Something to do with one of Dr Byville's patients,' responded Tracy, taking this as a question. 'He's gone over to Calleford for one of those funny Region Committee meetings this morning and can't be reached.'

'I think that'll be where Dr Meggie must be too,' murmured Shirley, who didn't like not to know what was going on and who wasn't above pretending that she did when she didn't. 'He's not in yet today either.'

'Well, old Merrylegs is certainly not over here,'

declared Tracy with spirit. 'Our Colin's been trying to get hold of him on the phone ever since he came in this morning.' She giggled. 'I said to him did he want me to try the "him and her" florists – without letting on to Bunty.'

'Dr Meggie told us he wouldn't be in,' said Shirley Partridge repressively. It was well known that Paul Meggie, made a widower a couple of years ago, was squiring a good-looking widow – and that his daughter, Bunty, wasn't happy about it. 'I'm surprised he didn't let your Dr Hulbert know, too.' She thoroughly disapproved of the use of either nicknames or the Christian names of the medical staff by anyone who wasn't a doctor and never encouraged it in others.

'At least he's not over at the Golden Nugget then,' said Tracy disrespectfully.

'Sorry, Tracy,' said Shirley, pursing her lips. 'I've got another call coming up.' The Golden Nugget was the non-medical staff's name for the clinic where all the local private medical and surgical work was done. 'Hello, caller . . . St Ninian's Hospital . . . Hatcher Ward? Hold the line, please . . .'

Holding the line was exactly what Dr Edwin Beaumont was trying to do at this moment. That he was trying to do it over the telephone did not help.

'What is the patient like now?' he asked with

a professional calm that was intended to be both exemplary and reassuring.

'Breathless, disorientated, and with a marked cyanosis,' said the young housewoman at the other end of the telephone line. Dilys Chomel knew perfectly well that she should have said 'dyspnoeic' instead of 'breathless' but to tell the truth she was feeling a bit short of breath on her own part just at this moment.

'I see.'

'I'm very sorry troubling you, sir, but I can't get hold of Dr Meggie either.' She consciously steadied herself against the desk in Sister Pocock's office. After all, she told herself firmly, she'd have to deal with her first death on the ward sometime if she was ever going to make the grade as a doctor. She just hadn't quite expected it to be this morning, that was all. 'It's a Mrs Muriel Galloway,' she said, 'and I've put her on oxygen and set up a saline drip just in case we need a line.'

'Good,' said Dr Beaumont in normal, everyday tones, also meant as an example of correct medical behaviour in times of stress.

'I didn't like her staring eyes,' hurried on the young housewoman, who in the heat of the moment had completely forgotten the medical synonym for that sign in a patient. She gulped and added naïvely, 'Or the way she's plucking at the bedclothes.'

'Floccilation,' said Dr Beaumont, who took his

teaching duties towards the newly qualified more seriously than did the absent Dr Byville, who was something of a cold fish.

'Oh . . .' Dilys Chomel remembered with surprise that she'd learned that that action by a patient was often a precursor of death not at medical college at all but at school in her English Literature lessons. 'Of course . . .'

Now she came to think about it, she realized that it had been William Shakespeare's description of the death of Sir John Falstaff which had been with her on the Women's Medical Ward while she regarded her own dying patient, not those stark clinical notes in her student textbooks. The poet and playwright had described the nose of the moribund Falstaff 'as sharp as a pen' and the 'smile upon his fingers' end' more memorably than any medical writer. 'Of course, sir, of course.'

'What is she on?' asked Dr Beaumont, who was only on call for Dr Byville and Dr Meggie while they were away from the two hospitals and naturally didn't have the Immortal Bard in his mind at this moment.

The housewoman reeled off a long list of medicaments.

'Give her an intramuscular diuretic *statim*,' instructed the senior doctor, more because it would give the girl something positive to do than aid a patient already beyond aid, 'and see that the relatives have been sent for.'

'Yes, sir,' said Dilys, adding, still surprised at what she had seen, 'and, sir, she's grasping at things that aren't there.'

'Carphology,' said Dr Beaumont briskly. 'We, on the other hand, my dear, are grasping at straws. Mrs Galloway's dying and you must tell the family so – and that we're very sorry but there's nothing more that we or anyone else can do for her now.'

'Yes, sir. Thank you, sir.' She paused and then said, 'Sir—'

'Yes?'

Dilys Chomel said uncertainly, 'I'm afraid there's something else, sir.'

'And what is that?' enquired Dr Beaumont with carefully controlled impatience.

'I understand that this patient – Mrs Muriel Galloway – was one of those taking part in Dr Meggie's Cardigan Protocol.'

'Hell and damnation,' said Dr Edwin Beaumont quite unprofessionally and without thinking at all.

Chapter Two

*The medical contention is, of course, that a bad doctor
is an impossibility.*

It wasn't only Dr Byville and Dr Meggie who were
not available at their hospitals.

'No, Dr Teal, I'm afraid Mr Maldonson isn't in
yet,' said Shirley Partridge for the third time that
morning.

She'd watched the lady doctor pacing up and
down the entrance hall of St Ninian's earlier on
looking tired and anxious and now she was back
on the phone again. It wasn't, Shirley Partridge knew
perfectly well, any obstetric emergency that was
bringing about all that stress. It was the unkind
behaviour of Mr Maldonson, her boss.

'Oh.' Dr Teal sounded drained. 'Oh . . . then I'll
have to . . . would you put me through to this
number, please?'

'Ringing now,' sang Shirley Partridge.

'And then,' said Marion Teal wearily, 'I think I'll

13

just come down to the front hall and wait for him to come in. It's not', she added more to herself than to the telephonist, 'as if there's anything more I can do here now anyway.'

The Obstetric Registrar, who had been on night duty all the week, was exhausted enough to have subsided on to one of the benches in the front hall and gone to sleep there and then but by now she was much too wound up to have done any such thing. Resting while you could was the action of someone with a quiet mind and Marion Teal's mind was not quiet. What she needed to do was to unload some of the bottled-up anger and irritation she was feeling over Mr Maldonson's blatant misogynism on someone somewhere – and preferably male.

The artist, Adrian Gomm, though admittedly of rather epicene appearance, was the nearest man. He was almost out of reach on a ladder.

'Do you mind,' she called up to him, 'if I ask you about your work?' It was more than Mr Maldonson ever did about hers. All he seemed interested in was making her so late going off-duty in the mornings that all her careful arrangements for child care were disrupted.

'Go ahead.'

'It's all very symbolic, isn't it?'

'That', said Gomm, 'is the general idea.'

'That's St Ninian at the top, isn't it?' The figure of a distinctly substantial saint clothed all over in white, complete with halo in gold, was spread across the whole of the upper part of the mural, his arms benevolently encompassing the painting.

'Top marks.'

Marion Teal flushed. 'But those other white gowns – the empty ones—'

'Yes?'

'I don't quite understand what they're doing in the painting.'

'Don't suppose you do,' said Adrian Gomm negligently from his perch above her.

'And they're all different,' persisted Marion. It was stupid to feel so disadvantaged just because she was having to look up at him. He wasn't even setting out to rattle her like Mr Maldonson did. Mr Maldonson did not like women in medicine – well, women in obstetric surgery anyway – and went out of his way to make that clear in every possible way.

'They are,' said Adrian Gomm laconically.

Marion Teal stepped back and regarded the mural more closely. 'This one below the saint on the left – that's an operation gown, surely?'

'It is.'

She frowned. 'But what I don't see is why its strings lead down to the long white gown lying on its side along the bottom.'

'Don't you?'

'More symbolism?' The white gown at the bottom of the mural was the opposite – almost a mirror

15

image – of the saint's one at the top of the mural. Whereas, though the arms of the saint stretched out and down, those of the gown down below stuck upwards in a stiff imploring fashion as if beseeching help.

'The underneath one's a shroud,' said Adrian Gomm, applying his brush to the wall.

'Oh . . . oh, I see.' She looked around. 'Then what about the other gown?'

'The one on the right?'

'Yes. Tell me, is that a straitjacket or something?' Dr Teal was hoping one day to become a Consultant Obstetrician and Gynaecologist – hence the importance of Mr Maldonson to her career prospects – not a psychiatrist, and hadn't actually ever set eyes on a straitjacket.

'That's symbolic, too,' said Adrian Gomm from somewhere level with her head. 'If you look carefully you can see that its strings tie into the saint's robes and the shroud, just like those on the operation gown do on the other side.'

'But what is it?' asked Marion, interested in spite of herself.

'Something called a sanbenito.' Gomm hitched up his paint-stained jeans.

'I've never heard of it,' she said, some of her preoccupation with Mr Maldonson fading.

'It was a robe worn by heretics,' Gomm informed her, 'before they were burned at the stake.'

16

Marion Teal shivered. Perhaps she was getting her own problems out of proportion.

'Although,' Adrian Gomm tightened his lips cynically, 'I dare say those in the operating gowns died without blessing often enough, too, don't you?'

'I wouldn't know about that,' she murmured, drifting back to the front door where she would be able to see Mr Maldonson come in.

If he did.

For Dr Martin Friar, on the other hand, the day was improving.

He had indeed diagnosed something interesting in the medical clinic he was taking for the absent Dr Meggie and, as the Out-Patient Department Sister had been sure he would, had brightened up quite markedly after doing so – and having had his coffee, of course.

'How long have you been feeling like this, Mrs Allison?' he asked the patient, a stout countrywoman from one of the more rural villages of Calleshire's hinterland.

Her answer confounded him.

''Bout since last Michaelmas, Doctor.'

'I see,' he murmured noncommittally. 'And then?'

'Then after Christmas the pain got worse. I was fair winded, too, every time I tried to do anything.'

'Housework, you mean?'

She stared at him. 'Well, that and seeing to the hens and geese. Got so that I couldn't bend to get the eggs, see? Not without the pain coming on.' She looked intently into Dr Friar's face, anxious that he should fully understand about her pain. 'Then, when I come to give m'husband a hand with the farrowing in the night, I came over really queer and we had to have the doctor out. Haven't done that since the children were young.'

'I see.' He made a note on the clean new record. He'd been brought up in the town himself and didn't really understand the urgencies of rural life.

'Then there was the shopping, doctor.'

'What about the shopping?' asked the registrar who didn't really understand that either.

'Carrying it, of course,' retorted Mrs Allison, for the moment quite forgetting to be over-awed by her surroundings. 'A week's shopping gets quite heavy, I can tell you. And it's a tidy step from the bus at Great Rooden up the hill to the farm after a morning on your feet at the market at Berebury.'

The registrar reached for his sphygmoman-ometer while Mrs Allison looked round the clinic, impressed and frightened in equal parts. It wasn't really intended to, but the Out-Patient Clinic sometimes had the same effect on those unfamiliar with it as the Hall of Justice in the Doge's Palace in Venice – walking the length of which was said to have concentrated the minds of those brought to trial there more than somewhat.

Dr Friar said, some of his own aching tiredness gone now, 'So that was when you got this feeling again, was it, Mrs Allison?'

'That's right,' she responded absently, her eyes on his hands. 'What are you going to do with that thing there, then?'

'Just putting it round your arm, that's all. It won't hurt.' He picked up his stethoscope. 'And then I'm going to have a listen to your ticker.'

"'T'ain't what it used to be,' she wheezed.

'No.'

'And my ankles swell something awful by night-time.'

'Yes, I'm sure they do.' Martin Friar glanced down at her bulging ankles and stout, lace-up shoes and made another note in her record. Her blood pressure was sky-high, of course. He didn't like the colour of Mrs Allison's lips either but he did not say so. Instead he asked, 'What are you like after a rest?'

'Rest?' She stared at him as if he was speaking another language. Then her face cleared. 'Oh, you mean Sundays, Doctor . . .'

He hadn't meant Sundays but he let her go on.

'Well, there's still always feeding the stock, of course, but I do put my feet up for a bit in the afternoons Sundays sometimes—'

Doctor and patient both regarded Mrs Allison's

swollen, pitted legs. She said, 'But it doesn't seem to make a lot of difference to the pain up here.'

'No.' Dr Friar nodded.

'That's why my own doctor thought I ought to come up to the hospital.'

'Quite right,' said the Senior Registrar, thinking – but not saying – that her own doctor – the old fool – should have sent her up to see them months ago. 'Because', he went on sedulously, 'I think we may be able to do something for you.'

'I didn't want to come, see,' she said again, not listening, 'because I've never been to hospital before.'

'One of your problems', said Martin Friar, not listening either, 'is that your arteries have got all furred up – a bit like an old water pipe does – and the blood can't flow through like it used to.'

Her face cleared. 'The water's terrible hard out our way, Doctor, and I do feel a great throbbing sometimes.'

'You will,' he said, not bothering to try to dispel her confusion. 'Now, what we need to do is to attempt to dissolve all the stuff that's stuck on the inside of your arteries without having to send you for an operation.'

'I shouldn't want to have an operation,' she said automatically.

'There are two treatments that we could give you,' said Dr Friar, ignoring this too. 'Actually, as it happens we're – that is, Dr Meggie is – testing one of the new ones here at St Ninian's.'

'Well, I never,' she said, suitably impressed.

'And what we'd really like to do, Mrs Allison, is to include you in one of our clinical trials by putting you on a course of one of these new tablets and seeing how you get on.'

She nodded uncomprehendingly.

'I shan't even know myself which one of the two drugs we're giving you,' said Martin Friar, adding with a winning smile, 'That's so I shan't be improperly influencing you in any way by what I say about the tablets when I prescribe them for you.'

'Thank you, Doctor,' she murmured, now even more mystified than ever. She'd come up to St Ninian's to be influenced and didn't understand why the doctor wasn't giving her something and saying how much good it would do her and that she'd soon be better again – like her own dear old doctor always did.

'It's called a double-blind trial,' Martin Friar was going on. He gave her his quick professional smile again – the one he'd been practising ever since he qualified – and said, 'Actually, to be quite accurate, it's called a prospective, non-randomized, double-blind crossover trial – not that you need to worry about the mechanics of that.'

'These tablets,' she said uncertainly, temporarily blinded by science and therefore concentrating on something she did understand, 'will they help this pain I've been having, then?'

'They might,' he said cautiously, adding, 'although I ought to warn you that they might just upset you a little, too. If they do, don't stop taking them. Come back and tell us here instead.'

'Yes, Doctor.'

Friar reached for a pre-packed bottle of tablets and wrote her name and a number on the label and entered both in a record book. 'Now, Mrs – er – Allison, isn't it? – I need you to sign this form.'

She fumbled in her handbag. 'I'm ever so sorry, Doctor. I didn't think to bring my reading spectacles with me.'

'That's all right,' he said easily. 'It's only just to say that I've explained to you all about this clinical trial we're doing and that you understand ... can you see the dotted line all right? Good. Well, just sign your name along that and Sister here will put her name there, too.'

'My ordinary writing?'

'Oh, yes,' he said, filling in his own part of the form to the effect that the patient's informed consent to taking part in a clinical trial had been obtained and a full explanation of possible risks and side-effects given. 'We'd like to see you here in another month, Mrs Allison. I may not be taking the clinic that day – it'll probably be Dr Meggie himself...'

She nodded. It had been Dr Meggie whom she'd come to see anyway.

'But when you come again, just remind him that you've been enrolled in the Cardigan Protocol, will you?'

'The Cardigan Protocol,' she repeated.

Dr Friar felt a pardonable sense of satisfaction with the outcome of the consultation. Mrs Allison was an ideal candidate for the new drug test and Dr Meggie would undoubtedly be pleased with him.

'Look,' he said to her, 'I'm putting a special marker in your notes to alert him when he sees you.'

Chapter Three

The rank and file of doctors are no more scientific than their tailors.

'God, that hurts!' shouted the young man in Berebury Hospital's spanking new Accident and Emergency Department. 'It hurts like hell.'

Darren Clements was lying outstretched on a couch in a curtained cubicle, his left arm surrounded by blood-soaked towels and his eyes wide open in an unhealthy combination of fear, anger and pain. Beads of sweat stood out on his forehead. There was also an element in his expression – often found in those who encounter really sizeable pain for the first time in their lives – of sheer surprise.

'I'm sorry, Mr Clements,' said Dr Dilys Chomel, who was the duty doctor on call for accidents and emergencies until Monday morning next, 'but your wound needs attention.'

The young man started as his gaze alighted on her advancing hands. He quickly jerked himself up on an elbow into a sitting position, pushing the towels away. 'What are you going to do with that needle?'

'I'm going to inject some local anaesthetic into the skin around the cut,' said Dilys Chomel, 'so that you won't feel the stitches going in.' Where she came from, young warriors of Darren Clements's age regularly sought pain that called for greater stoicism than this as part of their initiation to manhood rites. She regarded her patient not unsympathetically. 'That's a pretty nasty cut you've got there, you know.'

'Of course, I know,' snapped back the young man ungraciously, his naturally thin face sharpened by its owner's present anxious circumstances. 'My hand went right through their flaming glass roof. Watch it! You do know what you're doing, don't you? Ouch!'

'The X-rays don't show any glass left in the wound,' Dilys Chomel calmly continued with her suturing of the gaping skin, 'so you've been lucky there.'

'Lucky!' gasped Darren Clements. 'I'm going to get Gilroy's Pharmaceuticals for having unsafe glass in their roofs if it's the last thing I do.'

The lady doctor forbore to remark that if he'd fallen any further through the roof then that in itself might very well have been the last thing he did. Instead she said, 'And you haven't cut any tendons either. That would have meant either major sur-gery—'

He stiffened. 'I wouldn't have had it—'

'Or losing the use of your hand for the rest of your life,' finished Dr Chomel pleasantly. 'Can you turn it this way for me now, please?'

Darren Clements scowled mutinously but then pronated his injured wrist as asked.

'Even so, you might still need surgery,' continued the doctor. 'I'll do the best I can but you're going to have a scar there—'

'I'll keep it, thank you,' snapped Clements; like many another wounded in a good cause he wasn't averse to having evidence of this on his person.

'—which you may otherwise have to keep covered in case people attribute your cut wrist to a failed suicide attempt.' Dr Chomel bent forward again. 'Now turn the other side, please. This shouldn't hurt so much.'

Clements groaned but did as he was told. 'Are they still outside?'

'Who?'

'The police, of course,' he snarled. 'They want to know who was with me . . . and I'm not going to tell them.'

'And whoever it was,' she observed drily, 'as they aren't here, too, I take it that they were uninjured? Or did they just run away and leave you to face the music?'

'They escaped,' he said with dignity.

26

'And you were caught – you may feel this a little – red-handed?'

'That's the only reason they got me,' said Clements, missing her little joke. 'And for your information I felt that a lot.'

'Sorry. I'm nearly finished.'

'Besides,' he sniffed, 'I couldn't run anywhere with this hand. I'd have left a trail of blood a mile wide.' He winced as Dr Chomel inserted another suture. 'And even the police would be able to follow that.'

Dilys Chomel didn't know Calleshire well but even she had heard of Gilroy's Pharmaceuticals over at Staple St James. She sighed and asked with pity, 'What drugs are you on, then, my lad, might I ask?'

He stared at her, outraged. 'Drugs? I'm not on drugs.'

'You don't have to tell me,' she said punctiliously, 'but what were you doing trying to break into Gilroy's if you aren't on drugs?'

'Lighten up! I'm an animal rights activist, not a junkie.' As far as he was able, Darren Clements drew himself up and said with great impressment, 'We were going to try to let some of their monkeys loose.'

'No, Inspector,' George Gledhill, the Chief Chemist at Gilroy's, was saying at much the same time over at their works at Staple St James, 'none of them was released this time. The morons didn't get that far.'

'Good,' said Detective Inspector Sloan fervently. The last raid on Gilroy's by the Calleshire Animal Activists had resulted in monkeys infected with something with a long name that Sloan never did catch – but which sounded very nasty – being free to roam the countryside, carrying their disease with them. The police had had to catch the monkeys, though.

And fast.

'It's only thanks to that new alarm system we put in after last January', said Gledhill, 'that we foiled the blighters.' He was a short, square man, used to taking decisions.

'Glad to hear it, sir,' said Sloan, adding prosaically, 'You could say that prevention's better than cure in the police world as well as the medical one.'

Gledhill grinned. 'Don't tell the doctors but I don't know that it works for them. Just as well, probably, or I'd be out of a job.'

'I don't think you need worry, sir, not just yet. Any more than me.' Detective Inspector C. D. Sloan, known as Christopher Dennis to his wife and family, and for obvious reasons as 'Seedy' to his friends and colleagues in the Force, was the head of the tiny Criminal Investigation Department of 'F' Division of the Calleshire County Constabulary. Such crime as was committed in the country market town of Berebury and its environs landed up on his desk. 'I think there'll be work for us both, yet awhile.'

'Had a bit of trouble with the alarm system to begin with, though,' admitted Gledhill.

'Oh?' Sloan was sorry to hear that. The monkeys hadn't liked the cold weather the last time they had been free, that was for sure. 'The electrics?'

Gledhill shook his head. 'The monkeys. The little perishers found out how to set it off themselves. And did.'

'We're hoping to interview a man in connection with the attempted break-in,' said Sloan formally, 'later on this morning. I've got a constable waiting at the hospital now. I've just got to look in at Headquarters and then I'll be going over there myself.'

In the event it wasn't quite as simple as that. There was a message waiting for him at the police station. Superintendent Leeyes wanted to see him as soon as he got back.

'Ah, Sloan, there you are. Come in.' The superintendent looked up from his desk. 'And sit down. Something rather odd's just cropped up over at Berebury Hospital.'

'Sir?' said Sloan, conscious only that it was Friday and he'd been hoping to have a long-overdue weekend off.

'Of course, there may be nothing in it.'

'What would seem to be the trouble?' he asked, conscious of sounding rather like a doctor himself.

Leeyes waved a thin message sheet in the air. 'They've had a death up there this morning.'

'What sort of a death?' enquired Sloan warily. They must, after all, be used to deaths at the hospital: he understood that 'died or discharged' came under the same heading in their records. 'Not', he lifted an eyebrow, 'yet another of Mr Daniel McGrew's death-defying operations gone wrong, I trust?'

Superintendent Leeyes shook his head. 'No, not our careless neighbourhood cutter this time, thank goodness. It's a medical case.'

'Gone wrong, though?' asked Sloan pertinently.

'Can't say, Sloan. Not at this stage, anyway. Too soon to know.'

'And the trouble?' In Sloan's experience it was never too soon to know the exact nature of the trouble.

'A death, at least,' responded Leeyes, enigmatically. 'Of an old woman. But what the trouble is, Sloan, I can't rightly say yet.'

'Unexpected?' If there was a nub between those deaths which interested the police and those that didn't, then this was usually, but not always, it.

'No.'

'Then,' ventured Sloan, 'why us, sir?'

'Oh, no, Sloan,' Leeyes came back smartly. 'It's not as easy as that.'

It was never easy, thought Sloan, but he did not say so aloud. It wasn't worth it.

'Although', conceded the superintendent grudgingly, 'the relatives do all agree that they'd been warned ages ago that their mother was going to die. It's about the only thing', he added sourly, 'that they are agreed on.'

'So?' said Sloan. That could be good or bad.

'And been duly and properly sent for before she did die,' trumpeted Superintendent Leeyes. 'No grounds for complaint there.'

'I'm sorry, sir,' said Sloan, leaning forward in his chair, 'but I still don't quite see where we come into the picture.' Perhaps he would get his weekend off after all.

'I'm not at all sure that we do, Sloan,' barked Leeyes. 'That's the whole trouble. And you'll have to find out first, Sloan, if we do and she does.' He handed over the sheet of paper and added meaningfully, 'You and Detective Constable Crosby.'

'Yes, sir,' sighed Sloan. Constables – let alone detective constables – didn't come more jejune than Crosby of that ilk.

'Because', declared Leeyes ineluctably, 'if he's with you, then he's not here.'

'Quite so,' murmured Sloan.

'And I'm not having him underfoot in the station today a moment longer than I have to.'

'Thank you, sir,' said Sloan stiltedly. 'I understand. As it happens, he's over at the hospital now, taking a statement from an animal – er – liberator.'

31

Leeyes mumbled something very pithy about all activists of any shape, size and persuasion before going on, 'And find out if we are interested in the matter of this death at the hospital preferably before the deceased's son—' The superintendent rummaged about on his desk for another piece of paper. 'I've got the name here somewhere – ah, here we are – Gordon Galloway, son of Mrs Muriel Ethel Galloway.'

Detective Inspector Sloan gave an inward sigh and wrote both names down on a fresh page of his notebook as the prospect of his weekend off-duty faded.

'And find out,' repeated Superintendent Leeyes, 'before the precious Mr Gordon Galloway takes it into his head to go straight to either the Coroner or the press over our heads.'

'Like that, is it, sir?' observed Sloan thoughtfully. Either way could spell trouble: and both ways spelt even more trouble.

'What Mr Gordon Galloway wants, Sloan,' – Superintendent Leeyes rolled his eyes heavenwards – 'perish the thought, is action.'

'Yes, sir.' Just like the animal rights people, thought Sloan – but to himself.

'And he wants it now. If not sooner. He says,' – here the superintendent changed his tone to a parody of a self-important man – 'he's a businessman and that his time is valuable.'

'What is it exactly, sir, that he is – er – unhappy about?' asked Sloan, unimpressed. Businessmen who valued their own time – and nobody else's – were not unknown in the course of police enquiries. 'Do we know that at all?'

'The medical attention that his late mother got – or, rather, didn't get – in Berebury Hospital.'

'And is there any reason why that should be a matter for us?' persisted Sloan. Police time was valuable, too, although it wasn't fashionable to say so in the present social climate. 'They're usually quite good up there – except for Mr McGrew,' he added hastily. It wasn't for nothing that that particular surgeon was known throughout the county of Calleshire as Dangerous Dan.

'Mr Galloway alleges that the doctors were criminally negligent in their treatment of his late mother,' spelled out Leeyes.

'What? All of them?'

'Well, the House Physician mainly.'

Detective Inspector Sloan smoothed out the page of his notebook and said, 'On what grounds, precisely?'

'Four.'

'Four?' That sounded a bit overdone to Sloan.

'That's as far as I could make out,' the superintendent grunted. 'The fellow was a bit uptight.'

'Even so.'

'Firstly,' – Leeyes held up a finger as he started

to enumerate – 'the doctor who actually treated their mother on the ward is female – a Dr Dilys Chomel.'

Sloan didn't say anything. The superintendent's own misogynism was too much of a byword at the police station for any comment.

'Secondly,' – another finger came up beside the first – 'she is very young.'

They had just the same trouble in the Force with raw constables who got younger and younger every year. The unwanted Detective Constable Crosby was just such a case in point. He didn't even look the part, let alone act it. Perhaps Dr Chomel didn't either.

'Thirdly,' said Leeyes, continuing to recite Gordon Galloway's litany, 'Dr Chomel was wearing jeans.'

'Ah,' nodded Detective Inspector Sloan, veteran of many, many court proceedings, 'that won't have helped.'

'And fourthly,' said Leeyes, with the air of one playing a trump card, 'she isn't English.'

It was a close thing but, if anything, the superintendent's xenophobia exceeded his notable misogynism. All Sloan did was to glance studiously at the papers in his hand. 'It doesn't exactly amount to a hill of criminal beans, does it, sir?' he said at last.

'No,' conceded the superintendent with unexpected readiness, 'but wait for it, Sloan, wait for it . . .'

Sloan waited.

'But what Gordon Galloway didn't tell me and doesn't know – at least I don't think he does, unless it was him, of course – is that an hour after his mother died this morning we had an anonymous telephone call here at the station . . .'

'Did we, indeed?' murmured Sloan.

'Which our switchboard traced to a callbox near the hospital . . .'

Detective Inspector Sloan looked up.

'To the effect', went on Leeyes, 'that this woman, Muriel Galloway, had been entered in a drug trial when she was first admitted to the hospital.'

Sloan opened his notebook again.

The superintendent went on briskly, 'A drug trial that the unknown caller—'

'Male or female?'

'Female, switchboard thought but couldn't quite decide for certain. The voice sounded a bit muffled. Probably disguised through a handkerchief, they thought.'

Sloan made another note.

'A drug trial that the caller', finished Leeyes, effectively writing off Sloan's weekend off-duty once and for all, 'thought very dangerous indeed and might have killed her.'

Chapter Four

*The theory that every individual alive is of infinite value
is legislatively impractical.*

At first the Administrator at the Berebury Hospital
thought Detective Inspector Sloan and Detective
Constable Crosby had come about the perennial
thefts from the hospital kitchen, reported again and
again to the police.

'It's still going on, Inspector,' he complained. 'If
it's not from the stores, then it's from the kitchen
instead.' He grimaced. 'Proving it, of course, is a
horse of another colour.'

'That's true.' Sloan endorsed this with feeling. His
choice of villain there was one of the underchefs,
name of Dave: the one with the guileless baby-face.
Butter – and much else – was certainly melting away
somewhere even if it wasn't in the underchef's
mouth. 'But it's not about that.'

The Administrator, a man conditioned to bad
news, waited for the name of Mr Daniel McGrew to

be mentioned. 'Women's Medical?' he echoed, sounding surprised. 'That's the physicians. We don't usually have any—' He pulled himself together and said, 'Dr Byville and Dr Meggie have their beds there.'

'We'd rather like a word', said Sloan, deceptively low-key, 'with whoever had the late Mrs Muriel Galloway in their care.'

The Administrator pressed a button on the telephone on his desk and asked for Sister Pocock. 'Mrs Galloway was a patient of Dr Byville's,' he informed them a few minutes later, looking worried. 'He wasn't in earlier this morning and Dr Meggie was supposed to be on call for him—'

'Supposed?' Sloan picked up the salient word without difficulty.

'Apparently,' frowned the Administrator, 'no one has been able to get hold of Dr Meggie this morning so the ward contacted Dr Beaumont over at Kinnisport and he advised the House Physician before Mrs Galloway died.'

'Second reserve,' remarked Detective Constable Crosby, who was more interested in football than hospitals.

'And where was Dr Byville then?' asked Sloan, wishing that Crosby was the tiniest bit interested in detection as well.

'Oh,' the Administrator relaxed. 'He was over at Region – at Calleford, that is – making a presentation to the Drug Safety Committee meeting there.'

'Tell me more,' invited Sloan.

'Oh, not your sort of drug, Inspector,' said the Administrator, smiling quite kindly. 'Our sort of drug. We do quite a lot of medical drug trials here at Berebury for Gilroy's, the pharmaceutical people out at Staple St James – you'll know them, I dare say, Inspector.'

Sloan said he knew them all right.

'Ah, of course,' the man said. 'I was forgetting. The animal rights activists.'

'Very active, they are, some of them,' contributed Crosby, who had taken an unrepentant statement from Darren Clements. 'Not to mention the monkeys. They're pretty nippy, too.'

'We don't have any responsibility for the – er – work done on the animals there,' said the Administrator, 'but . . .'

'But?' said Sloan encouragingly.

'But we are naturally concerned with the observing of the strict guidelines for any clinical trials we do here.'

'Naturally.'

'So—'

'So we'd like a word with Dr Roger Byville,' said Sloan blandly.

'Sister Pocock says he's back now.'

'If he can spare us a moment,' murmured Sloan, still low-key.

Dr Byville, at least, was not deceived by this deceptively diffident approach. But not over-awed either. In fact he was quite brisk.

'Muriel Galloway?' he said, quite composed. 'Her cause of death, Inspector, was exactly as I certified. There were no doubts in my mind when I signed the death certificate and there are none now.'

The policeman murmured something indistinct – and unspecific – about unhappy relatives.

'In my opinion,' responded Byville without hesitation, 'there were no clinical grounds for holding a *post mortem*.' He looked meaningfully at Detective Inspector Sloan and went on, 'Nor, as far as I am aware, were there any other reasons.' The specialist's glance rested briefly on Detective Constable Crosby's youthful visage before he turned back to face Sloan, saying interrogatively, 'There may, of course, be other factors of which I am unaware.'

Sloan did not answer the question directly. Instead he said, 'And it did not seem to you, then, Doctor, a death to be reported to the Coroner?'

'Certainly not,' returned Byville robustly. 'No suspicious circumstances had been reported to me; the patient had been in hospital for over a week before she died; there had been no anaesthetic or surgical intervention – what else could there possibly have been to justify referral?'

'I couldn't say—' began Sloan.

But the physician hadn't finished. 'Nor had the

woman been starving herself to death before she came into hospital or anything like that.'

'No,' agreed Detective Inspector Sloan mildly.

'Nothing but natural causes,' asserted Dr Byville with undiminished vigour.

'And you had no reason to suppose that Mrs Galloway's death was in any way related to any medical procedure or treatment she had been receiving?'

'Quite the contrary, Inspector,' rejoined the physician smoothly. 'I can assure you that but for the treatment that she had been having, she'd have died months – if not years – ago. Mrs Galloway had been in congestive heart failure for a long time.'

'I see, Doctor.' Detective Inspector Sloan paused, his notebook open and his pen at the ready. 'And did that treatment by any chance happen to include a new drug that was being tested on the patient?'

Dr Byville looked up sharply and gave a short, cold laugh. 'Oh, so that's what's worrying you, is it? Yes, Inspector, Muriel Galloway had been entered for a clinical trial. Nearly all the heart patients here have. There's no secret about that.'

'A clinical trial . . . ' Detective Inspector Sloan wrote that down. It was other sorts of trials that came more easily to his mind but he was always ready to learn.

'A clinical trial, Inspector,' swept on the consultant dispassionately, 'given the code name of "Cardigan", properly set up and approved by both the

Regional and Hospital Ethics Committees and con-
ducted by the cardiologist over at Kinnisport, Dr
Meggie, in accordance with a strict protocol laid
down by them—'

'Ah,' said Sloan, making another note.

'—on a compound supplied by Messrs Gilroy
(Berebury) Ltd, a pharmaceutical company at Staple
St James, no doubt,' – he tightened his lips – 'known
to you as well as to the animal rights vandals.'

'This new drug, Doctor,' said Sloan, forbearing to
mention the trouble that the police – as well as
Gilroy's – to say nothing of the monkeys, who had
found that freedom palled – had had there, too, 'that
you were experimenting on Mrs Galloway with—'

'Testing, Inspector,' intervened Byville, looking
pained. 'Testing. The experiments are done on
animals.'

'Testing, then,' amended Sloan, whose object was
not the bandying of words.

'I can assure you that her being entered for the
Cardigan Protocol didn't make any difference to her
dying. She was going to do that anyway.'

Detective Constable Crosby turned to the physician and said innocently, 'So it didn't save her
either, then?'

'No,' said Roger Byville shortly. 'I'm afraid not.'

Detective Inspector Sloan, policeman first and
policeman last, put a rather more important question to the doctor. 'Or accelerate her death?'

'In my opinion, no. Not even if she was given it in the first place. I couldn't say about that, of course.'

'You don't know?'

'No,' said Byville.

'But you said—'

'What I said, Inspector,' said Byville coldly, 'was that Muriel Galloway was taking part in the clinical trial.'

'So?'

'So she may not actually have been given the drug.'

'You mean', said Sloan, light dawning, 'that there would have been dummy tablets—'

'I mean', countered the doctor firmly, 'that any proper protocol naturally contains matched controls.'

'So Mrs Galloway might have been having only harmless tablets?' This, Sloan realized, was going to take some explaining to the superintendent.

'Inert would be a better description than harmless, Inspector,' remarked the doctor.

'Inert,' conceded Sloan between clenched teeth. 'So she might only have been having inert tablets—'

'She might.'

'Well?'

'On the other hand,' said Byville precisely, 'she might not.'

Sloan's teeth were now so tightly clenched that he was surprised the others couldn't hear them grinding.

'Do you toss for it?' enquired Detective Constable Crosby with every sign of genuine interest. 'Heads you get the real stuff, tails you don't?'

Dr Roger Byville didn't look as if he'd ever tossed anything more than a pancake and that a long time ago. 'Matched controls', he said stiffly, 'are selected every bit as carefully as test cases.'

Sloan didn't like test cases in law. He didn't know anything about medical ones; but he was beginning to think he wasn't going to like them either. 'But surely, Doctor,' he said, 'withholding a life-saving new drug could be potentially harmful, too.'

'Oh, yes, indeed. That's quite different,' said the specialist readily. 'Once we are really certain that it is effective, then it would be quite unethical to withhold it from all sufferers.'

'So?'

'So then,' said Roger Byville immediately, 'the comparison trials with the matched controls would be abandoned forthwith and the new drug given to all patients with the condition from then on.'

'How do you tell?' asked Crosby.

Dr Byville smiled thinly. 'It's not always very easy.'

'This new drug—' began Sloan, going back to his notebook.

'Provisionally called Cardigan,' supplied Byville.

'Tell me about it,' invited Sloan, hoping that the doctor's words wouldn't be long ones.

Dr Byville visibly relaxed while he expounded on what they hoped to gain from the medicinal properties of the drug called Cardigan. 'It's got a compound number, too, Inspector – these things are all done by computer these days. There's no room for sheer inspiration any more but more than that I can't tell you.' He smiled thinly. 'It's not my baby, you see.'

Sloan nodded his understanding. Almost everything at the police station had a number and was done by computer these days, too, but they hadn't yet found a mechanical substitute for the smell of malfeasance somewhere.

Or the nose that could sniff it out.

Sometimes, of course.

Not always.

He wasn't sure about the smell – if there was one – of anything here yet.

Any more than he knew if the 'leaning on the gate' approach to problem-solving was better than feeding everything under the sun into a computer and pressing a few keys.

Dr Byville was still talking. 'But, gentlemen, you'd do better talking to the real expert. Naturally, Dr Paul Meggie as the Consultant Cardiologist to the Hospital Trust is the doctor in overall charge of the Cardigan Protocol.'

Unfortunately, reported the Hospital Administrator regretfully after a further twenty minutes on the telephone, Dr Meggie was not available for interview. No one, it presently transpired – that is, when they'd cut their way through the Administrator's circumlocutory manner of speaking – was quite sure exactly where Dr Paul Meggie was.

The person who was missing Dr Paul Meggie most of all at this moment – and that rather to his own surprise – was his registrar.

In the first instance Dr Martin Friar had welcomed the opportunity of taking his consultant's clinic single-handed, then he had positively relished responding to a call from Barnesdale Ward about a case that could have been bacterial endocarditis. In Dr Meggie's absence he had pontificated, prescribed and prognosticated – in fact, generally fulfilled the role of clinical specialist to which he so keenly aspired.

It was different now.

He had just been settling nicely into this agreeable mode when there was a call from a general practitioner out in the country. Dr Angus Browne wanted Dr Meggie to do an urgent domiciliary visit to see a Mr Abel Granger and made it quite clear that as Dr Meggie couldn't be contacted, he, Dr Friar, would have to come instead.

That was when Martin Friar's difficulties had started.

'Larking?' he said. 'Where's Larking?'

'Take the Cullingoak Road from Kinnisport and then second left after the pub,' said Dr Browne. 'Willow End Farm's up a track on your right. Mind you keep right when it forks or you'll end up in the stream. I'll be at the house – the patient's too ill to move or leave.'

'But—'

'I've promised the family a second opinion,' said the general practitioner a trifle testily, 'and I need it now. Tomorrow will be too late.'

'I'll be there,' promised Friar. 'No problem.'

But there was a problem when he got there.

Not knowing what to do with his hands was only part of it. There was, of course, absolutely nothing Martin Friar could do with them. The registrar was having his first experience of watching a man dying in his own bed without the benefit of hospital support. It was, he soon realized, he – Martin Friar – not the patient, who was missing the benefit of hospital support. There was no hiding in Sister's office or behind Dr Meggie here. The man was beyond aid and that was all there was to it.

What Friar did have was the experience of watching a really skilled general practitioner at work in a domestic setting. Standing in a large farmhouse kitchen, round a big table scrubbed to bare-bone whiteness, was a silent anxious family, hanging on Martin Friar's every word but still looking to their father's own doctor – the man they knew and trusted – for real comfort. He could learn a lot, he decided, from listening to Dr Angus Browne.

'Remarkable man, their father,' the family doctor was saying in front of the adult children. The patient's wife was where she'd been for the last seven days and nights – by her husband's bedside. 'Built this farm up from nothing.'

The elder son nodded.

'He's had good home nursing, too,' said the local doctor. 'Everything he needed.'

A daughter caught her breath.

'A king couldn't have had better care than he's had,' asserted Angus Browne. An historian might have suspected irony here since various monarchs had been subjected to medical treatments that could only have added to their discomfort and accelerated their demise, but the patient's family took this pronouncement at its face value and were reassured.

Martin Friar nodded gravely. Several kings that he knew about would have kept their thrones a lot longer had the same attention been paid to their electrolyte levels as it had to those of the old farmer upstairs but this was not the time to say so.

'It's Mother I'm worried about,' said the younger son. 'She hasn't had her clothes off for nearly a week now.'

Angus Browne said sapiently, 'She'll no' thank you for taking her away from your father now.'

'But, Doctor,' protested the younger son, her favourite, 'she'll collapse if she goes on like this.'

The general practitioner shook his head and said with the wisdom of long experience, 'She'll no' collapse, Christopher, all the while your father needs her. I can tell you that.' He paused and then added significantly, 'And it won't be for long now, will it, Dr Friar?'

Martin Friar looked solemn. 'I'm afraid not.'

'So Dad's nearly at the end of the road, is he?' asked Simon, the elder son, his own role at the farm about to change significantly and new duties begin.

'He's had a good innings,' responded Browne obliquely, 'but I think they'll be drawing stumps, soon.' He turned politely to the quondam consultant and said, 'Don't you, Dr Friar?'

Martin Friar nodded gravely. It was about the only thing he could do.

'Although,' said Angus Browne, automatically hedging his bets, 'the heart has a remarkable capacity for keeping going.'

The younger son found his tongue again. And was surprised to find how dry it was. 'When . . .' he licked his lips. 'I mean . . . can you say how long?'

'Not long now,' said Browne gently, as they all heard the sound of another, rather noisier, car coming up the farm lane.

'That'll be the rector,' said the daughter, taking

off her apron and hurrying through the house. 'We'd better get the front door open, hadn't we?'

Dr Browne led Martin Friar out of the back door as the representative of the next world came in at the front one – the seldom-opened farmhouse front door that the coffin would be going out of very soon.

'Thanks for coming,' Browne said when they were well out of earshot.

'There was nothing I could do.'

'Oh, yes, there was,' said Angus Browne unexpectedly. 'Now you've seen the patient for yourself, you can go back and tell your boss that I don't like this new drug he's peddling one little bit.'

Chapter Five

Doctors have their uses, real as well as imaginary.

Over in the village of Staple St James, Dr Paul Meggie had also been noted as an absentee by Gilroy Pharmaceuticals (Berebury) Ltd.

'Sorry about this, Al,' said George Gledhill, their Chief Chemist. 'He wanted you to meet him while you were over here.'

'These medical bods do tend to get held up more than some,' replied Al Dexter easily. He was Head of Dexter Palindome (Luston) plc, manufacturing chemists, and liked other people to get off on the wrong foot anyway. 'Can't be helped.'

'Oh, he'll be along all right, never worry,' contributed Mike Itchen, Deputy Chief Chemist and resident boffin at Gilroy's, in the laid-back manner he was cultivating so assiduously. 'He's keen.' Behind the laid-back manner were the research brains of Gilroy's.

Al Dexter took another sip of his pre-luncheon

drink. 'Trouble is, you can't ever check up on the medics. All they've got to say is that they've had an emergency call.'

'True.' George Gledhill glanced at his watch. 'All the same, I don't think we'll wait to eat.'

He pushed his chair back. Doctors with a penchant for drug research could be recruited for clinical programmes without difficulty – for a fee, of course. Good cooks were more tricky to come by and trickier still to keep – fee or no fee. The cook at Gilroy's was first class and all of their visitors enjoyed her cooking. Most of them relished the corporate dining room at the Hall, too, and Gledhill was happy to note that their guest had every appearance of a man who hadn't seen his toes for quite a while.

'Fine with me,' said Al Dexter automatically. 'Glad you yourselves could make it on time anyway. Sounds as if you've had a busy morning, both of you.'

'We've got people looking at the roof now,' said the Chief Chemist indirectly. 'They were lucky not to get themselves killed, silly young fools.'

'If that's all they were,' remarked Dexter, 'then you haven't anything to worry about, have you?'

'The Health and Safety Executive for starters and the insurance people . . .' began Mike Itchen, who was a worrier.

'I mean', explained Dexter, 'that if it was only the

monkeys they were after, you don't have problems, do you?'

Gledhill looked up sharply. 'You think they might have been real burglars?'

'It's what I would have been worried about,' said Al Dexter. He didn't have the look of a man who worried about anything. 'Good cover for getting in – animal rights – if you were looking for something, don't you think?'

Gledhill and Itchen carefully avoided looking at each other.

'In my experience,' Dexter added authoritatively, 'people are prepared to believe anything about animal rights activists.'

'We'll look into it,' said Itchen in the neutral tones he favoured these days. He had an expression that was similarly blank.

'You're still working on Naomite surely,' said Dexter, 'aren't you?'

Gledhill looked round quickly as if someone else might have been listening. 'It's only in the embryo stage, Al,' he said. 'Nothing doing there at all yet.'

'Sure,' said Dexter comfortably, 'but they don't know that, do they?'

'And nothing doing at the Ethics Committee at Region this morning either,' added Itchen gloomily. 'We only had one submission and it got the chop.'

A different sort of ethic prevailed as Al Dexter

studiously avoided enquiring about the form of Gilroy's new submission. He was here with other fish to fry and if the two chemists wanted to tell him about their firm's newest compound then they would tell him fast enough. And if they didn't, then he, Al Dexter, didn't really want to know.

'Just like Byville's last effort,' said the Chief Chemist regretfully. 'He's a trier, though, I'll give the man that.'

Dexter raised an enquiring eyebrow.

'They wouldn't wear our APX 125 trials, Al.' George Gledhill shook his head. 'A great pity, especially as Byville was so keen to test the refined compound. Said he's nearly there with some really good "effect-size" figures.'

'Byville's no good with committees,' pronounced Itchen weightily. 'Puts their backs up as soon as he opens his mouth.'

'He's really into spleens, though,' said Gledhill. 'Been making quite a speciality of treating them lately. We might have something for you there one day, Al.'

'But he's no good with people,' insisted Mike Itchen, still brooding about the committee meeting. 'Doesn't see that he's got to convince the Safety of Drugs Committee before he gets anywhere,' – he sniffed – 'for all that he wants to examine everyone in Calleshire without a spleen. And', he added mordantly, 'some with.'

'If you can corner the market,' said Al Dexter simply, 'then you should.' It was the spirit that made millionaires.

'It's all right for you,' said Mike Itchen.

Dexter Palindome (Luston) plc weren't research chemists, but manufacturing ones. They didn't have to waste their substance on research-and-development programmes which got through money like water. They merely processed what the boffins thought worth making, leaving the risk business to others. Their highest-paid employees weren't research chemists at all but production engineers and marketing men.

'I don't think anyone's aiming to corner the market,' said George Gledhill piously. He didn't add that with patents and licences this was hardly necessary these days. 'With Roger Byville it's more of an interest.'

'And', said Itchen, 'it's not such a crowded field as some.'

'I guess Joe Public doesn't really understand the spleen,' said Al Dexter.

'You can say that again,' said Mike Itchen, who found the lay members of the Ethics Committee the most difficult of all to deal with. Give him a scientist any day. Unless he could have a businessman, of course.

'So what', asked Dexter curiously, 'didn't they like about the APX 125 trials, then?'

'Everything,' said the Chief Chemist, rising to his feet rather abruptly. 'Come on, let's eat.'

A curious mixture of altruism and business acumen had led the founding fathers of the firm of Gilroy Pharmaceuticals (and they were men only now just starting their retirement) to buy a large, empty Victorian mansion. It was a time when large, empty Victorian mansions were something of a drug on the post-war housing market.

'The dining room's straight ahead,' Mike Itchen reminded Dexter.

It would certainly have been a misnomer to call it a canteen. The Hall at Staple St James had not been quite stately enough for preservation and had been converted into offices and research laboratories well before the Victorian revivalists had been sufficiently interested or organized enough to protest.

'Some eating place you've got here,' said Dexter, suitably impressed by a painted ceiling reminiscent of the worst excesses of the French neo-classical period.

'Built to last, did the Victorians,' said Mike Itchen with his first show of enthusiasm.

'We've found a use for almost everything here except the maze,' said George Gledhill proudly, going into his set party piece for visitors. 'You name it and we've got it here. Stables, ice-house, game larder, laundry, greenhouses, cellars . . . you'll have a little of this white Burgundy won't you, Al? . . . lake, grotto . . .'

'What on earth's a grotto?'

'It's where the bad man of the garden lived. You know – before the era of something nasty in the woodshed came in.' Gledhill looked preternaturally solemn. 'No real old garden was complete without a hermit.'

'You don't say.' Al Dexter went back to a topic he found more interesting. 'Say, do you people get much hassle from these ethics committees of yours?'

Mike Itchen frowned. 'It all depends.'

'On the face of the guy putting the product forward?' suggested Al, since human nature is the same the world over. 'Or other things?'

'Well, Al,' temporized Itchen, 'you know yourself what committees are like.'

'Sure,' said Al Dexter untruthfully. There were no committees built into the corporate structure of Dexter Palindome (Luston) plc. The decision-making process was delegated to a nail-biting level; bucks stopped as far down the management pyramid as possible and all potentially unprofitable work was headed off at the pass long before it got on to anyone's time-sheet.

'They're the very devil,' admitted the Chief Chemist since he was talking to a contractor and not a business rival. 'How it can be OK to let thousands suffer and die from some untreatable condition and all wrong for one poor sod—'

'Who was going to die anyway,' contributed Mike Itchen cynically.

'—to snuff it while we're using him to try to find a cure for the same thing beats me.'

'It's an unfair world,' agreed Al Dexter ambiguously.

'In the first place,' grumbled Gledhill, still sore from this morning's rejection, 'the Ethics Committee's always so totally negative.'

'It's not their product, of course,' contributed Al Dexter reasonably.

'And as for the Safety of Medicines people . . .' carried on Gledhill.

'Never a breath of enthusiasm there,' seconded his deputy.

'That's their whole trouble,' said Gledhill. 'All they want to do is keep their noses clean.'

'And what they don't like', said Mike Itchen, 'is criticism. Can't take a breath of the stuff.'

They didn't come more worldly than Al Dexter. 'They don't have anything riding on success, that's the difference.'

The Chief Chemist shrugged. 'True.'

'And you fellows have', said Dexter simply; he pronounced the word with relish: 'Cardigan.'

Gledhill's face lit up suddenly. 'I'll say we have. And so has Dr Paul – fresh carnation buttonhole –

Meggie. Wherever the old fox's got to this morning.'

Detective Constable Crosby drew a neat line in his notebook after talking to the luckless Darren Clements in the Accident and Emergency Department. He hadn't got very far. That young man was clearly prepared for martyrdom rather than disclose the names of his confederates.

'Me, shop my mates?' he'd said. 'You must be joking. Catch 'em yourself.'

'I dare say we will,' replied Crosby equably. 'We caught the monkeys all right last time and your lot aren't as clever.'

He found Dr Dilys Chomel more co-operative, although she wasn't herself making a lot of sense of her interview with the detective constable. For one thing she was still rather confused and for another the policeman wasn't making himself very clear.

'You had an old lady here this morning, miss, on Women's Medical in heart failure—' Crosby had taken a unilateral decision about addressing any young woman with hair like rats' tails as 'Doctor'.

'Mrs Galloway?' said Dilys, who hadn't really reckoned on having the police in on her first death. 'Yes. She died, of course ... I mean.' She halted in mid-speech. She had just realized that she was sounding like the woman in the children's verse who had swallowed a fly and worked her way up to swallowing a horse. She, too, had died, of course. The House Physician started again. 'I mean,' she said haltingly, 'naturally she died. She was very, very ill.'

'Ah, that's what we wanted to know.' Detective Constable Crosby made a new entry in his notebook. 'You say she died naturally?'

'That, too,' said the young lady doctor drily, wondering if she would ever truly master the manifold intricacies of the English language.

'Did you attempt resuscitation?'

'No.'

Detective Constable Crosby said ponderously, 'Not to attempt resuscitation when you can, miss, is murder.'

'No, it isn't.' She shook her head and said, 'It's not to resuscitate when you should that's murder.'

This much she did know. Dilys Chomel had paid particular attention to her medical ethics lectures since in her own home country in Africa a very different view was taken of almost all such situations. Especially the survival of girl babies born to families who wanted only sons.

'Deciding not to resuscitate makes the doctor into judge, jury and executioner,' persisted Crosby, who didn't like hospitals anyway.

'That's euthanasia,' said Dilys Chomel firmly, deciding, since the policeman seemed a bit strong on ethics, not to reveal Dr Paul Meggie's simple rule on resuscitating the terminally ill or very elderly. Detective Constable Crosby, she sensed, might not like it.

This unwritten procedure had been spelled out to her by her predecessor in the house officer's job when she took it over. 'You don't', he'd said meaningfully, 'do it without consulting Dr Meggie first, understood?'

'But', she'd protested, 'you've only got half a minute. By the time I've located Dr Meggie, the patient'll be dead.'

'Got it in one, haven't you?' he'd murmured, giving her a pitying look before going off to climb the next rung of the uncertain ladder that comprised the greasy pole of his medical career.

They took a very different view of the care of the elderly, too, in the far country from which Dilys Chomel had come.

They cherished them.

'The Coroner,' Detective Constable Crosby was saying at his stateliest, 'has ordered a *post-mortem* examination at the request of the police.'

'The consultant—' began Dilys. In hospitals, consultants ranked directly under the Almighty.

'The Coroner', repeated Crosby, 'has ordered a *post-mortem* examination.' In the eyes of the police force the Coroner represented the Crown and thus easily outranked chief constables as well as hospital consultants. 'And I've come to enquire into the whereabouts of the body of the deceased.'

'If it hasn't been released to the relatives,' said Dilys, 'then it'll be over in the Potter's Field.'

'Come again, miss?'

'Sorry.' She tossed her head. 'It's what the staff here call the mortuary. Most hospitals, you see, have a private name for their mortuary so that the staff can mention it without upsetting the patients. Didn't you know, Constable?'

Upsetting their clients wasn't one of their worries down at the police station. There – like it or not – they called the charge room the charge room. Crosby still looked puzzled. 'The Potter's Field, did you say, miss?'

'It's from the Bible.' A missionary culture had done well by Dr Chomel. 'You'll find it in St Matthew's Gospel.'

'I still don't see—'

'The Potter's Field was where they buried strangers,' explained Dilys Chomel. 'Mrs Muriel Galloway's body'll be there if it's still in the hospital.'

It was.

And, the mortuary attendant promised Detective Constable Crosby, it would be sent over to Dr Dabbe, the Consultant Pathologist, for a *post mortem* without delay.

Crosby thanked him and was just about to take his departure when the man asked him if Dr Meggie had turned up yet. It wasn't like him, the mortuary

attendant said, not to be at one or other of the hospitals, throwing his weight about as usual.

'Not yet,' said the detective constable, 'but I
expect he will.'

"Im and his perishing buttonhole,' said the man.
'Who does he think he is?'

'God,' said Crosby simply. 'They all do.'

Chapter Six

Doctors if no better than other men are certainly no worse.

'Thanks for talking to my housewoman about that congestive heart failure on Women's Medical over at Berebury this morning,' murmured Roger Byville as he found himself standing just behind Dr Beaumont in the antiquated lift at St Ninian's Hospital. He'd already forgotten the patient's name. 'It's her first house job and she's still very new here.'

'No trouble,' said Beaumont politely, 'although there was nothing to be done, I'm afraid.'

The lift creaked to a standstill at the first floor and two nurses and a pathology technician got out.

'The family are kicking up a bit of a stink all the same,' said Byville now that the two doctors were alone together.

'Are they?' Dr Edwin Beaumont inclined his head sympathetically. It was the relatives of Mr Daniel McGrew's patients who usually did that.

Pour cause.

Byville said, punching the lift button with quite unnecessary force, 'They're asking for a *post mortem.'*

'That should put their minds at rest.'

'I hope it does.' Byville gave an unamused laugh. 'They've already been to the police.'

Dr Beaumont raised his eyebrows and decided against getting out of the lift at the floor which he'd been heading for. 'On what grounds?' he asked carefully, as they continued upwards.

'God knows.' Byville grimaced. 'The next thing they'll be doing is talking to the local newspaper. The editor would enjoy that.'

'It would be a great pity,' observed Edwin Beaumont in his usual measured way.

'It would.' In contrast with most of the other consultants on the staff of the two hospitals, Roger Byville was a controlled, rather colourless man, but even he sounded heated now. 'St Ninian's gets quite enough bad publicity as it is from the antics of that maniac, McGrew. We don't need any more.'

Dr Edwin Beaumont glanced at the lift indicator and sighed. 'Our Dan doesn't exactly help the healing image, does he?'

Byville scowled. 'I can never see why the surgical people don't shop him. I would. Gives the whole place – let alone the profession – a bad name.'

'Not our headache, though,' said Beaumont, one physician to another, and unmindful, too, of

Edmund Burke's famous dictum that for evil to flourish it was only necessary that good men do nothing.

'Thank God it isn't,' said Byville.

'I've heard,' advanced Beaumont cautiously, 'that even the Three Wise Men don't know what to do about him next.'

'I never did hold with that idea.' Roger Byville sniffed contemptuously. 'Catch someone as egocentric as Dangerous Dan being told by three of his professional colleagues—' It was well known that Daniel McGrew didn't admit to having peers. '—that he's not doing his job properly—'

'Well—'

'And then his pulling his socks up. I don't know about you, but I don't call that likely, myself.'

'Quite,' agreed Dr Beaumont, although that wasn't the way in which he himself would have described the remit of the three distinguished surgeons who were summoned when a Calleshire consultant showed signs of what were euphemistically described as 'human failings'. 'Quite,' he said again.

'And I still don't see why', grumbled Byville, 'I should have to pay whopping insurance premiums for medical defence just to keep clowns like McGrew out of trouble.'

'No, Roger.' Beaumont paused and then with more relevance than was perhaps tactful said, 'This heart failure of yours—'

'Yes?'

'Is it going to mean', asked Beaumont delicately, 'trouble?'

'Not if I can help it,' responded Byville. 'Oh, I know she was on Paul's Cardigan Protocol but that wasn't what killed her.'

'No, no, I'm sure,' said Beaumont hastily.

'And I told that detective inspector so.'

'Paul isn't going to like it, though, all the same.'

'No, he isn't.' Byville nodded his agreement to this. 'Not one little bit. He's very keen on his precious test results for Cardigan is our Paul.'

That, decided Dr Beaumont, was one way of putting it but he did not say so aloud.

Roger Byville looked up as at long last the old lift wheezed to a halt at the top floor of St Ninian's. 'Got a moment to spare yourself, Edwin? I've got an interesting spleen on Lorkyn Ward. Come and have a look at him with me, if you've time. A young man of twenty-five, who's been ill for two weeks. He insisted on being shipped over here from Berebury so the family could visit . . . I'm afraid he's not doing very well.'

'That you, Shirl?' The land-line from Berebury on the St Ninian's switchboard sprang to life. 'Tracy here.'

Shirley Partridge completed a telephone connection to Barnesdale Ward and then spoke to Berebury Hospital. 'Who did you say? Oh, Dr Meggie?' She shifted her head to get a better look at the attendance board. 'No, Tracy, he's still not in.'

'There's someone here who wants to see him,' announced Tracy with relish.

'I'm afraid they're going to be unlucky then,' retorted Shirley. 'Sorry.'

'Something to do with Female Medical.'

'They want him, do they?'

'No. Not them,' said Tracy, savouring the exchange. 'It's the police who want him. They're on their way over to St Ninian's now.'

'I'll tell them when they arrive,' promised Shirley who was almost as skilled as the medical profession at playing down simple human drama.

'They're hoping to see him straight away,' persisted Tracy.

'That might be more difficult,' said Shirley Partridge, pursing her lips. 'Seems as if everyone wants to talk to him today and nobody knows where he is. He hasn't left word and I've tried all the usual places. And I can't raise Miss Meggie either.'

'Have you tried the golf course?' suggested Tracy slyly.

Bunty Meggie, the doctor's daughter, having done her stint as telephone minder ever since her mother's death, had been released from her servitude by the advent of the mobile telephone.

'Or the Merry Widow,' added Tracy, tongue in cheek. 'He might still be with her.'

Shirley Partridge flushed. 'Not in the middle of the morning,' she said primly.

'If you ask me,' said Tracy frankly, 'she's not the sort to be seen before twelve. Half a ton of make-up takes a bit of putting on.'

'Was there anything else?' asked Shirley, who, had she known it, was with Siegfried Sassoon in the matter of not liking those who 'talked lightly of his deathless friends'.

'There's a patient over at the Golden Nugget raising Cain', reported Tracy, 'because old Merrylegs hasn't been in there to see her yet.'

'Is it something serious?'

Tracy gave a snort. 'I'll say it is. If she isn't discharged in time she'll have to pay the fees for another night in there and that's not chicken feed.'

'Oh, dear.' Shirley Partridge sounded quite worried. Dr Meggie's private practice was near and dear to him. That it also cost the patients very dear didn't weigh with her at all. 'That's not like him,' she said carefully.

'It isn't.' Tracy endorsed this with more vigour than was really kind.

'Not if he said he would be there,' said Shirley loyally.

*

Not only was Dr Meggie not to be found at any of the hospitals – that much Detective Inspector Sloan had quickly established – but it soon transpired that he had missed an important lunchtime engagement at Gilroy's Pharmaceuticals at Staple St James.

'Important?' queried Sloan rather sharply. Policemen worked in a field where luncheon was lucky if you got it but only incidental to work, not part of it.

'That's what their Chief Chemist told me, Inspector,' said Dr Meggie's clinical secretary, a little nervously. 'Mr Gledhill sounded quite put out when he rang. I understand they'd got someone over from Luston specially to meet him.'

'Perhaps Dr Meggie just forgot.'

'Never.' Although clearly flustered the secretary drew herself up and said, 'Besides, I reminded him myself yesterday.'

'So the engagement was in his diary?' said Sloan.

'It was in mine,' she said astringently, pointing to her desk. 'Dr Meggie was expected over at Staple St James at one o'clock after his clinic.'

'For lunch?' Detective Inspector Sloan and Detective Constable Crosby had not eaten yet.

'I understand', she said, 'it was to discuss the progress of the Cardigan Protocol over a meal.'

'All right. A working lunch.'

The secretary indicated an empty in-tray on her desk. 'He always took the computer print-out of the results home with him at night.'

Sloan didn't like computers.

'You see,' she hesitated, 'he's always very careful about confidentiality.'

'Yes, miss.' Sloan could have wished, though, that Dr Meggie wasn't being quite so secretive about his own whereabouts today. He, Sloan, had promised an old gardening friend that he would drive over to Cullingoak tomorrow to admire his friend's new greenhouse rose.

The rose was called 'Celeste'. It was in full flower now and it wasn't even the middle of May yet, and its scent was said to be quite memorable.

At the present moment the disappearance of Dr Paul Meggie had a less attractive smell and distinct overtones of the *Marie Celeste*; which was something very different.

He made a note of the doctor's home address. 'Come along, Crosby.'

Just as a single twist of a kaleidoscope changes the picture but keeps the same constituents, so the death that day of old Abel Granger at Willow End Farm, Larking, brought about a new arrangement in the dispositions of his immediate family.

Old Mrs Granger, who had encountered death before, folded her husband's hands across his still chest, closed his eyes and drew her best Egyptian cotton sheet over the face that had been her constant companion for the best part of fifty years. Simon, the elder son, went off to telephone Dr Angus Browne and Morton & Sons, the Berebury undertakers, while the daughter tried to persuade her mother to rest.

Christopher Granger, the younger son, to whom death so far had been a stranger, drew on his boots, whistled for his dog and went outside. It was more breathing space than fresh air that he felt he needed but the land makes its own demands on those who live by it and he set out to make a conscientious – if rather overdue – survey of the family's acres. There were some bullocks being fattened in the Thither field which always needed a weather eye kept on them. If they could find a way out of their pasture, then find it they would.

The further he walked the better Christopher began to feel. He'd have to face his mother later on, of course. He half hoped she wouldn't break down when she saw him and he half hoped she would – he didn't really know what to hope. What he did know was that he wasn't in any hurry to go back indoors. His sister would be bustling about and Simon would be busy doing all the right things. All he wanted to do was to have a quiet think.

He called his dog and decided to walk home along the lower – the longer – path, the one that ran alongside the stream and through the willow copse.

That was when he saw the car.

It was on the track that led to the gate and he thought that he could hear the engine running.

He quickened his pace. Someone coming up to the farm – the undertaker, perhaps – it looked a smart enough car to be the undertaker's – they made a lot more money than farmers did these days – must have taken the wrong track at the fork. A lot of drivers did that if they didn't know the way to the farmhouse. He'd go down and open the gate. You couldn't turn a car there otherwise; not with the stream on one side and a drainage leat on the other.

As he got nearer he was more sure still that he could hear the car's engine running so he waved to the driver. He must have only just come that way.

'Wait there,' he called out. 'I'll have to open the gate for you.'

The man at the wheel made no response. He seemed to be leaning forward studying the dashboard.

Christopher Granger advanced curiously, his dog at his heel.

The farmer's son might until today have been something of a stranger to human death but his acquaintanceship with it was being rapidly extended.

That this man was dead, Granger was never in any doubt at all after he had seen him. It wasn't so much the appearance of the body that convinced him as the fact that there was a length of flexible tubing leading from the exhaust pipe to the almost closed window behind the driver's seat.

Without thinking Christopher Granger opened the driver's door and slipped his hand inside the car to turn off the engine. As he did so the man's body canted over the door sill towards him. He fielded the dead weight quite as automatically and expertly as if it had been that of a sheep. As he did so his eye was caught by a boldly labelled document folder lying on the passenger seat beside the dead man.

Re-energized and shaking slightly in a way that his country-bred mother would have called 'shreuggly', Christopher Granger made his way back to Willow End farmhouse very quickly indeed.

The words 'Cardigan Protocol' written on the label of the document folder meant nothing to him at all.

Then.

Chapter Seven

That instrument of torture, the night bell.

'You've done what?' barked Superintendent Leeyes down the telephone line from Berebury Police Station to St Ninian's Hospital at Kinnisport.

'Found Dr Meggie,' repeated Sloan.

'And about time, too,' grumbled Leeyes. 'You've been looking for him all morning and that should be long enough.'

'Dead,' said Sloan.

'I've had that man Gordon Galloway on to me again about his mother,' complained the superintendent. He stopped suddenly. 'What was that you said, Sloan?'

'Dr Meggie's been found dead, sir.'

'He has, has he—'

'In his car.'

'Find the car, find the man,' said Leeyes sententiously.

'With a tube leading from the exhaust pipe.'

74

'Any note?'

'One hasn't been found,' said Sloan precisely. 'Only a file with the results of some drug trials he's been working on.'

'Remorse?' suggested Leeyes with interest.

'Too soon to say, sir.'

'Not, mind you, that I think any of 'em feel it. Knocked out of them all at medical school, if you ask me.'

'Very probably, sir.' He cleared his throat. 'We're leaving for Larking now.' He had chosen his words with accuracy. If Crosby drove there as fast as he usually did then there was no guarantee that they would get there in one piece; or even that they would arrive at Willow End Farm at all.

'Don't let Crosby play whacky races on the way there,' said Leeyes. 'Police cars come expensive.'

'I'll try,' promised Sloan, adding, 'Of course, sir, Dr Meggie's death may be quite unconnected with Mrs Galloway's.'

'Find out.'

'Dr Byville', volunteered Sloan, 'seemed unconcerned enough about her when we spoke to him at Berebury.'

'Nothing at all to go by,' said Leeyes darkly. 'Remember, Sloan, that doctors get so used to people dying on their hands that they carry it off quite differently from normal people.'

'He did tell us that Mrs Galloway was going to die anyway,' pointed out Sloan.

'Well, he would, wouldn't he?' retorted the superintendent unanswerably. 'What you mustn't forget, Sloan, is that anonymous call we had here at the station saying the old lady had been treated with something funny. There's nothing routine about that—'

'I won't forget, sir,' Sloan promised – and the very next minute did just that.

He forgot absolutely everything as Detective Constable Crosby took the wheel of the police car and proceeded to put it through its paces on roads designed for haywains.

A single twist of the kaleidoscope changed the whole picture for Dr Martin Friar, too. Until he heard the news about Dr Meggie, the Senior Registrar at Kinnisport Hospital had been feeling pretty upbeat.

This was because he had had a stimulating – not to say thoroughly revivifying – exchange with Adrian Gomm, the artist at work on the mural in the front hall of the hospital.

'Can't exactly say that I can see what you're getting at,' he'd called up to the man as he paused on his way to Lorkyn Ward to examine the work in progress.

The artist, who had the sort of long hair that

brought out the worst in other men, had shrugged his shoulders and replied offensively, 'Don't suppose you do.'

'Aren't I meant to, then?'

'It's up to you.' Adrian Gomm kept his back to the registrar and carried on painting. 'There's plenty of meaning in it for those that can see.'

There was certainly plenty to look at in the half-completed mural in which the endless towering arches after the style of Giambattista Piranesi were challenged by dislocation after the manner of Maurits Cornelis Escher.

Martin Friar, as affronted as the next man at the suggestion that he might not possess the seeing eye of the true art connoisseur, squinted up between the artist's legs and said provocatively, 'Looks like all the Circles of Hell to me.'

'It's meant to,' came the short reply.

'Beauty being in the eye of the beholder and all that?' hazarded the doctor.

'Beauty?' At the mention of the word, Adrian Gomm turned to face the registrar, laying aside his brush and regarding Martin Friar with a belligerence surprising in one so epicene in appearance. 'Beauty? In case you don't know, this is a hospital not a pleasure garden. There's no beauty here. You should know that. You work here, don't you?' He peered down at him from his working platform. 'I'm sure I've seen you around.'

'Too right, I do,' said the registrar feelingly. 'And how.'

Adrian Gomm glared at him. 'You're not the brute who's driving that lady doctor to despair, are you? Coming in late every morning on purpose to make her late. Because if so, let me tell you—'

'No, no,' said Friar hastily. 'That's Mr Maldonson.'

'Well, if you've found any beauty here in St Ninian's,' challenged the artist, 'leaving aside that lady doctor, Mrs Teal, then you're a better man than I am. If you ask me, this whole grotty outfit should have been pulled down years ago.'

'Maternity,' returned the doctor, thinking quickly. 'There's beauty in putting a newborn baby into its mother's arms. It makes her beautiful, too, however plain she is,' he added, surprising himself that he'd noticed and remembered.

'That's Nature not Medicine,' retorted Gomm. 'You lot can't go grabbing the credit for Nature, although I've noticed you usually do.' He turned his back on Friar unceremoniously and resumed his work, saying over his shoulder, 'If you look carefully down there, you'll see I've given Nature full marks.'

Martin Friar obediently cast his eyes towards the bottom of the colourful mural and said, 'Worms?'

'One of the medical trials and tribulations of Job,' returned Adrian Gomm, who appeared to be concentrating on an almond-shaped outline at the top right of the wall.

'Ah, so you're bringing religion in, are you?' asked Dr Friar.

'No holds barred in art, you know.' Gomm wiped a sticky hand across his forehead. 'I've got complete artistic freedom here – wouldn't have touched the job otherwise – any more than you'd let someone else tell you what to prescribe for one of your patients.'

'So what are you putting in that ellipse thing, then?'

'It's called a mandorla,' said Gomm. 'And I'm painting Christus Medicus in it, if you really want to know.'

'Are you indeed?' murmured Friar.

'God as the Physician of his People.' Gomm jerked a shoulder towards the left-hand side of his mural and went on, 'That's the scientific side over there but I'm still working on it.'

'So I see.'

'There's something else, too, about what I'm doing on this wall.'

'What's that?'

'This mural'll still be here when all your work's dead and buried.' The artist took an appraising look at his work. 'And people will still be looking for meaning in it. Some of them', he added gratuitously, this time wiping his hands on his paint-stained jeans, 'will find it, too.'

'All right, all right, I get the message.' The registrar started to go on his way and then halted, his eye caught by the representation of a sinister crouching figure in the bottom left-hand corner of the mural. It was half animal, half man: a hairy devil with horns and cloven hoofs but with a human face. Dr Martin Friar could have sworn – it couldn't only be his imagination, surely? – that the face was meant to be that of the Senior Surgeon at St Ninian's, Mr Daniel McGrew.

'Dad dead?'

The young woman who had answered the policemen's knock on the front door of a detached house on the outskirts of Kinnisport was still wearing her golfing clothes.

'I'm afraid so, miss.'

Bunty Meggie sat now very still on a settee in the sitting room while Detective Inspector Sloan and Detective Constable Crosby talked to her, her knee-length culottes and monogrammed sports shirt looking oddly out of place in the well-appointed, rather austere room.

She looked from one policeman to the other. 'Are you trying to tell me that there's been an accident?'

'No, miss,' said Sloan. That much at least was certain.

She shook her head as if to brush away the news. 'Not an accident?'

'No, miss. I'm sorry to have to tell you that your father's been found dead in his car.' That it had been Dr Meggie's car by the stream at Willow End Farm had been one of the easier things to confirm. Crosby had done it straightaway.

'Well, then—' said the young woman quickly.

'With a tube leading from the exhaust pipe into the car,' said Sloan.

'And the engine still running,' supplemented Crosby helpfully.

Bunty Meggie suddenly clenched her fists, her face crumpling. She burst out, 'That woman! It's her. I know it is!'

'What woman, miss?' If there was one thing that Detective Inspector Sloan had learned it was when to produce a notebook and when not to. This was one of the times when he left it out of sight.

'She's driven him to it,' wailed Bunty Meggie. 'I knew she would.'

'Who?' prompted Sloan.

'She made him choose between us,' she said tightly. 'Oh, she was very clever, the devil.'

'Who, miss?' said Sloan again.

'Oh, poor Dad!' Bunty Meggie started to rock to and fro. 'I should have known it would have been all too much for him.'

'Should you, miss?'

'I was to go, you see.' She looked Sloan full in the face. 'She didn't care where.'

'Go, miss? Where?'

'Anywhere.' She burst into uncontrollable, ungainly sobs, embarrassing to see. 'Oh, poor Dad. He couldn't take it. She was wicked, wicked.'

'I shall need to know who, miss.'

'Mrs Glawari.' The girl gulped. 'She wanted me to call her Hannah but I wouldn't. I always called her Mrs Glawari and she didn't like it.'

'And who is Mrs Hannah Glawari?' persisted Sloan, although he was beginning to think he could guess.

'The woman who wanted to come here,' she said fiercely, 'and lord it over my mother's house.'

Sloan nodded, light having dawned.

'I wouldn't let her call Dad "Paul" either – not when she was talking to me.' She choked. 'I gave up everything to come home and look after Dad when my mother died and she . . . she . . . wanted to take it all away from me.'

'By marrying Dr Meggie?' said Sloan.

She nodded, quite beyond speech now.

'So—' began Sloan, but he was interrupted by Detective Constable Crosby who was leaning forward unusually eager to say something.

'So,' Crosby delivered his line with great emphasis, 'when did you last see your father then?'

The girl turned a blotched face to him and sniffed, the historical allusion quite lost on her. 'Yesterday evening.'

'Not at breakfast?'

She shook her head. 'No, I didn't see him then. He had a call early this morning. The telephone bell woke me.'

'How early?'

She brushed a lock of dishevelled hair away from her eyes. 'It must have been about five o'clock, I suppose. It was nearly light. After a bit I heard his car go out and I went back to sleep again.'

'And then?' prompted Sloan. Crosby had transferred his attention to some silver trophies in a glass cabinet on the other side of the room.

'Then,' she said, 'when I did get up, I went off to play in a golf competition. My partner and I were due to be first off the tee.'

'Was your father in the habit of getting emergency calls in the night like that?'

'Oh, yes. He didn't get them often, just every now and then,' she said readily. 'This was to a farm somewhere out Larking way. I don't remember the name.'

'How did you know that?'

'The address was scribbled on the pad by his bed,' she said. 'I found it when I made his bed. It's still there.'

'I take it, then,' said the detective inspector, 'that when your father didn't come home you phoned Kinnisport Hospital to say that Dr Meggie wouldn't be taking his clinic there this morning?'

Bunty Meggie looked up at that and shook her head. 'No, I didn't, Inspector. He'd have left me a note if he wanted me to do that. He always did.'

Chapter Eight

Nothing is more dangerous than a poor doctor.

Over at Gilroy's Pharmaceuticals at Staple St James the Chief Chemist, his deputy, and their public relations specialist were locked in conference. George Gledhill and Mike Itchen were agonizing over the best way to handle the news of the break-in at the pharmaceutical firm by the Calleshire Animal Activists. Pamela Gallop, their in-house expert, was telling them what that way was and not getting very far. Damage limitation is seldom popular.

'Activists!' snorted George Gledhill, going over old ground. 'I shouldn't have thought they could have activated a fruit machine. Not a brain between them.'

'If we could be sure of that,' said Itchen meaningfully, 'then we'd really be getting somewhere, wouldn't we?'

'And what you advise then, Pamela, is that we forget the break-in?' said George Gledhill, unwilling to acknowledge Itchen's point. 'From a public-relations point of view, I mean.'

'Dignified silence and all that?' Mike Itchen put in his pennyworth.

'I think that would be best for us,' contributed their specialist. 'After all, we're not looking for lost monkeys this time, are we?'

There was a corporate shudder at the memory of last time. That had been when the press had hinted at green monkey disease.

'We should play it down as much as we can,' added Pamela briefly. 'It's not good news.'

Mike Itchen nodded his agreement. 'The less said about it the better, if you ask me.'

'The police', growled Gledhill, 'will do their charging whether we like it or not.'

Pamela Gallop tapped her file. 'I owe the editor of the Berebury paper a lunch.'

'Breaking and entering, I suppose it'll be,' said Itchen, sounding worldly wise. It was part of his credo not to be surprised by anything these days.

'They broke the roof,' said Gledhill flatly, 'and Darren Clements entered the hard way.'

'The stringers', continued Pamela, ploughing a rather lonely furrow, 'won't pick it up if it's not in the local newspaper in the first place. And by the time any case comes to court it'll have all blown over.'

'But, Pamela—'

'Press reports put ideas into other people's heads,' said Pamela Gallop, belatedly remembering that it was her usual job at Gilroy's Pharmaceuticals to do just that. 'You never can tell where they'll lead—'

She broke off as a secretary entered the room in haste.

'I'm sorry, Mr Gledhill,' began the girl breathlessly, 'but Dr Meggie's secretary's just been on the phone.'

'I should think so,' said Gledhill roundly. 'What's his story?'

'It's not like that, Mr Gledhill,' said the girl, wide eyed. 'He's been found dead in his car. They think it's carbon monoxide poisoning.'

'Strewth!' exploded Mike Itchen, quite forgetting his commitment to a cool urbanity. 'What on earth did he want to go and do that for?'

'And she said to tell you', went on the girl conscientiously, 'that Dr Meggie had the Cardigan Protocol papers with him when . . .' She faltered. 'When it happened. The police have taken charge of them.'

Pamela Gallop was not the only one to note that the news was received by both the Chief Chemist and his deputy with a regret tempered by acute anxiety.

The flick of the kaleidoscope changed the whole future for Mrs Hannah Glawari, too.

She sat now in the rigid stillness of shock in her pretty little sitting room in one of the early Victorian houses down by St Faith's Church, overlooking the old market place. Detective Inspector Sloan was aware that he wasn't meant to notice the fine tremor in her hands that she was doing her best to conceal. The quaver in her voice was more difficult to keep hidden.

'Poor, poor Paul,' she said. 'He was torn, Inspector. Very torn. I could see that. Bunty is so terribly possessive of her father.'

'Daughters are,' said Sloan, who only had a son.

'But he needed me, too.'

'Yes, madam.'

'There are things, Inspector, that a daughter can't do and Bunty just didn't understand that.'

'No, madam,' said Sloan. He was busy keeping one eye on Detective Constable Crosby who was altogether too precariously perched on a chintz pouffe. Crosby seemed too big for the room let alone the pouffe.

'And a man in Paul's position', said Mrs Glawari tremulously, 'needs a wife.'

Sloan nodded. It was too soon to know if a lady in Hannah Glawari's position needed a husband. He suspected that this might be the case.

A faraway look came into her eyes. 'In some ways, Inspector, he was still a young man.'

'Yes, madam, I'm sure.' By the time Detective

Inspector Sloan had seen Dr Paul Meggie he was looking a very old man indeed but he had to admit that that was nothing to go by.

'And he cared for me.' Her voice was much more quavery now.

'I'm sure, madam,' said Sloan neutrally. Even he could take in the difference between this very feminine room and the more Spartan spareness of the Meggie household. There hadn't seemed too much stress on home comforts there.

There was an even more marked difference between this petite, well-groomed and sympathetically dressed woman and Bunty Meggie's sturdy sportive figure and practical clothes. Sloan could guess whom an extrovert image-conscious medical consultant might prefer at his side in public. And in private, too, very probably.

'I know that Paul cared for me.' Mrs Glawari twisted a ring on her left fourth finger and gazed at it thoughtfully. 'He said so all the time. Besides—'

'Besides?' said Sloan. If Crosby fell off that pouffe he'd have his guts for garters.

'Besides a woman always knows, Inspector. Always.'

'I'm sure, madam.' His own wife, Margaret, knew because he told her so. Always.

Detective Constable Crosby had seemed at first unsure of what to do with his knees. Turning them first one way and then another, he had settled for enveloping his long arms round them and then locking his fingers together. He unclasped a hand now to point at a photograph in a silver frame.

'That him, is it?' he asked conversationally.

Hannah Glawari expelled her breath in a long, tearful sigh. 'Yes, that's my Paul.'

Only, decided Sloan, he wasn't her Paul any longer. He'd died as Bunty Meggie's father and presumably that was all. He braced himself to put a painful question to the distressed woman. 'Forgive me, madam, but was – er – marriage – er – contemplated?'

'We were to be married on Midsummer's Day, Inspector. Paul said it would be a good time because we were both in the mid-summer of our lives.' Here she broke down completely, quite beyond speech now.

Shaking off a powerful charm, Sloan made a swift return to his duties. As they left Hannah Glawari's house he said to the detective constable, 'Crosby, find out who Dr Meggie's solicitors are.'

'Sir?'

'And enquire whether the good doctor had by any chance made a will in expectation of marriage before he died or a new one, for that matter.'

'Beg pardon, sir, but why would that be?'

'Because you can't sue a dead man for breach of promise,' said Sloan irritably. 'That's why.'

*

'Driving a man to suicide, Sloan,' pronounced Super-intendent Leeyes weightily, 'isn't an offence yet.'

'No, sir,' Detective Inspector Sloan had, duty bound, reported back at Berebury Police Station before going over to the *post mortem* on Dr Meggie.

'Although,' – Leeyes stroked his chin consideringly – 'I'm not at all sure that it shouldn't be.'

'Yes, sir. One day, perhaps.' There were a number of actions that were both legal and bad. His own mother, who was a great churchwoman, was strong on sin and weak on parking offences. 'Actually, sir, we're not one hundred per cent certain yet about the suicide in Dr Meggie's case.'

'Ha!'

'His daughter says', here Sloan chose his words with extreme care, 'that her father had a telephone call about five o'clock this morning asking him to go to see a patient at Willow End Farm at Larking.'

'Did he?' said Leeyes, adding significantly, 'And did she?'

'There's an old farmer there by the name of Granger who was very ill and, in fact, did die there later on today from heart failure.'

'That's three deaths,' said Leeyes.

'Yes, sir,' agreed Sloan. From all accounts it was the merest chance that there hadn't been four. Dr Dilys Chomel had told Crosby that the glass that had injured Darren Clements's hand and arm had been perilously near an artery.

'I'm glad you haven't forgotten the woman in Berebury Hospital,' said Leeyes tartly.

'No, sir. I haven't forgotten her. Or her son. I'm seeing Mr Gordon Galloway later on this afternoon. After we've heard what Dr Dabbe has to say about his mother.'

'Willow End Farm, Larking,' mused the superintendent, changing tack again. 'That's where the doctor was found, isn't it?'

'Yes, sir.' Sloan coughed. 'Only he wasn't sent for.'

'What's that?' The superintendent's head came up with a jerk. 'What do you mean?'

'According to their statements neither the farmer's family – the Grangers – nor the patient's own doctor – that's Angus Browne – telephoned Dr Meggie at five o'clock this morning to ask him to visit Abel Granger.' He turned a page in his notebook. 'Dr Browne did ring for him but not until later on in the morning.'

'Puts things in a different light, that,' conceded Leeyes upon the instant.

'It means', ventured Sloan, 'that whoever did send that message—'

'Or says that the message had been sent.'

'That's something we'll be looking into, sir.' Sloan accepted his superior officer's qualification without demur. 'What it does mean is that whoever did cause that message to be written on the pad beside the deceased's bed' – he didn't think he could put it more precisely than that – 'knew that old Abel Granger was ill enough to warrant the consultant being called out at that time.'

'And that Dr Meggie knew that too,' put in Leeyes, 'and would come if sent for. Doctors don't always.'

'He'd go all right, sir.' Sloan told the superintendent that Dr Browne had said that old Abel Granger – like Mrs Muriel Galloway – had been one of those entered for the trial of the drug code-named Cardigan.

Leeyes drummed his fingers on his desk. 'I don't like it, Sloan.'

'No, sir.' Sloan hadn't thought for one moment that he would. He added something else the superintendent wouldn't like either. 'Someone telephoned Kinnisport Hospital first thing this morning to say Dr Meggie wouldn't be taking his clinic there today and—'

'And?'

'And Bunty Meggie – that's the deceased's daughter – swears it wasn't her.'

Shirley Partridge, who had taken the incoming call on her switchboard, had been sure it had been a woman on the line and she had told Detective Constable Crosby so. 'The voice was a bit husky,' she said, 'as if she might have had a cold.' That was all she remembered.

'But was it the doctor's daughter?' Crosby had insisted. He had reached Shirley's little glass-walled cubicle at Kinnisport Hospital only after a bruising encounter in the entrance hall with the artist, Adrian Gomm.

Of this she had been less sure.

'Think back,' he urged.

'I don't know Miss Meggie's voice very well,' said Shirley Partridge, professionally challenged. 'She doesn't often ring the hospital. Not since Dr Meggie got his own mobile telephone.'

'But someone rang,' persisted the young constable.

'Oh, yes.' Shirley Partridge had been quite confident about this. 'And I took the message and passed it on straightaway to Dr Friar. He was the one who needed to know about taking the clinic instead of Dr Meggie, you see.'

Crosby's expression suddenly became very cunning. 'Did the caller ask for Dr Friar by name or did you just ring through to him yourself? Off your own bat, I mean.'

'She said would I pass a message on to Dr Friar.'

'But she didn't ask to be put through to him himself?' asked Crosby, who had never really mastered the matter of leading questions.

'No.'

'And when exactly did the call come?'

Shirley Partridge sank her head into her hands. 'I'd have to think.'

'Do that,' commanded Crosby. 'It's quite important.'

'You could always ask Dr Friar.'

'I have,' said Crosby. Dr Martin Friar, having been woken by the call, had immediately gone back to sleep. He had no idea when the telephone had rung.

'It was early,' she volunteered.

'How early?'

'Quite early.'

'Was there anyone about? That funny chap doing the painting, say?'

'Only Dr Teal. She kept on coming along here after she came off-duty at seven thirty.'

'Did this woman ring before or after you saw Dr Teal?'

'Oh, before,' said Shirley Partridge, her face clearing. 'She rang even before the calls for Niobe started to come in and they're always early.'

'Who's Niobe?' asked Crosby.

'It's not a person. It's the name of one of the wards here. At least,' – Shirley Partridge remembered something – 'I think Niobe was a person in history. All the wards here, you see, are named after doctors in history—'

'And Niobe was a doctor?'

'No.' She shook her head. 'But when they wanted

95

a name for a new sort of ward in the hospital some-one suggested they called it Niobe.'

'Why?'

'Niobe is the ward here where they treat infer-tility—'

'So?'

'Niobe is someone in Greek mythology who wept for her babies that were not . . . Dr Teal explained it to me.'

Crosby turned slightly pink.

'And the ladies', said Shirley, 'who are to be admitted there have to take their temperatures early in the morning so they know whether to come in that day.'

Crosby turned even more pink.

'Because, you see, it all depends on—' but she was talking to thin air.

Detective Constable Crosby had fled.

Chapter Nine

Make it compulsory for a doctor using a brass plate to have inscribed in it . . . the words 'Remember, I too am mortal.'

One of the many things which Dr Dilys Chomel found difficult about being a house physician at Berebury Hospital Trust was the sudden switches of role required of her.

One moment there she was happily dispensing authoritative advice to patients and having people twice her age hanging on her every word. The next minute she was trotting along behind Dr Byville, being cut down to size by having her every suggestion about diagnosis and treatment subjected to comment and criticism. Teaching by humiliation it was known in the profession.

And all the time she was trying to keep on the good side of Sister Pocock who had been ruling the Women's Medical Ward longer than anyone could remember and whose goodwill made all the difference to a quiet life.

Life at the moment was not quiet.

'Is there anyone else on this ward who's on the Cardigan Protocol?' Dr Byville had heard the news about Dr Meggie and hurried straight back to the Women's Medical Ward at Berebury Hospital.

'The ventricular fibrillation in bed seven.' The patient in bed seven had a name but Dilys Chomel had forgotten it and she doubted if Dr Byville had ever known it.

'God knows what all this is about,' said Byville irritably, 'but I don't like it.'

'No, sir.' Dilys Chomel had never liked the Cardigan Protocol but no one had ever asked her opinion.

'And what Meggie wanted to go and do a thing like that for—' It was the nearest Dilys Chomel had ever been to seeing Roger Byville animated. A normally colourless man, he was quite stirred now.

'No, sir.' Where Dilys Chomel came from suicide was not a problem. Keeping alive took up too much time and energy.

'Start taking the ventricular fibrillation off the protocol,' ordered the senior physician, 'and step up her other drugs to compensate if necessary.'

'Very good, sir.'

'But be very careful. There could just be some problems with Cardigan that we don't know about.'

'I understand.'

The consultant relaxed for a moment. 'I reckon', he said unguardedly, 'that all hell's going to be let loose over this.'

'Yes, sir,' said Dilys. 'Do we ... I mean, is there something that—'

He cut her short abruptly. 'Anyone else on it here?'

'No, sir,' stammered Dilys. 'Not since Mrs Galloway died.'

He jerked his head. 'Anything back from the pathologist about her yet?'

Dilys Chomel shook her head. 'Not so far, sir.'

'See that I get it as soon as it comes.' Dr Roger Byville looked up and down the ward. 'You'd better give me a run-down on all of Dr Meggie's cases here. I'll have to take them over until they find someone else to fill his post and that isn't going to be easy.'

Dilys obediently supplied him with the details and then came back to the condition of one of Dr Byville's own patients on the ward. 'I'm a bit worried about Mrs Aileen Hathersage – she's the spleen in the end bed—'

He gave a quick frown. 'Spleens are always worrying. Has she got any Howell-Jolly bodies?'

'I don't know, sir,' she said haltingly, trying hard to remember what Howell-Jolly bodies were. Something seen in blood, she knew, but she couldn't for the life of her think what. She wished she dare get out her little *vade mecum* from her pocket and look it – or was it them? – up.

'Find out,' commanded Byville. 'What's the trouble with her now, anyway?'

'I'm not sure, sir. Only that she's rather ill today.' Naïve as she was, Dilys Chomel had already learned all about the meiosis of medical-speak: doctor to doctor, that is. It was understatement raised to an art form. In that context 'rather ill' meant what the lay person would consider very ill indeed. By the same token, 'not too good' really meant dying. 'She's quite a lot worse', continued Dilys uncomfortably, 'than she was yesterday.'

Byville gave an almost imperceptible shrug of his thin shoulders. 'She had a splenectomy for some reason or other last year.'

'It was ruptured in a road traffic accident,' said Dilys, who had clerked the patient on her admission. 'They couldn't stop it bleeding.'

'So,' the consultant opened his hands in a gesture of hopelessness, 'she's lost her spleen. And now she needs it. Pretty badly, actually.'

'Yes, sir, I know but—'

'And, Dr Chomel, neither you nor I can put it back for her.'

'No, sir, of course not.'

'I expect the barber boys'll find a way of doing it one day but not yet awhile.'

'No, sir.' Sister Pocock had had to explain to her

why Dr Byville always called the surgeons the barber boys. Ever since then Dilys had been scanning the streets of Berebury looking for a red-and-white-striped barber's pole. Sister Pocock had also attempted – without success – to make her understand why it was that the physicians invariably considered themselves a cut above the surgeons.

'And Mrs Hathersage will have been very prone to infection ever since.'

'I understand that, sir, but—'

'And will remain so for the rest of her life. Some authorities', he said, belatedly conscious of a duty to teach, 'maintain that the immunity improves with time but I have yet to see the evidence of that myself.'

Greatly daring, Dilys Chomel said, 'I'm afraid what we're giving her doesn't seem to be doing her much good.'

'I don't suppose it is,' said Byville dispassionately.

'But—'

'Most of these people', said Byville, a medical nihilist if ever there was one, 'die from an overwhelming infection.'

'She's just not responding,' said Dilys worriedly.

'A mild infection in a person without a spleen progresses to a major one very quickly. That's her trouble—' He broke off as his call-pager started bleeping. 'You'd better tell the husband I'll talk to him. After he's visited her, mind you, not before. That's something you'll soon learn, Dr Chomel. Not to give bad news before the relatives see the patient. Tell 'em on their way out and let them have time to sleep on it and get their faces straight before they visit again.'

'Thank you, sir—'

But Dr Byville was already on his mobile telephone. 'Gledhill? Hello, yes, I've heard. It's bad news, all right. What's that? Right, I'll come over to you now.' He turned back to Dilys. 'I'm going to Gilroy's at Staple St James. If you can't get hold of me, ring Martin Friar at Kinnisport. He'll have to stand in for Paul over there.'

Dr Dabbe, the Consultant Pathologist at Berebury, welcomed Detective Inspector Sloan and Detective Constable Crosby to his domain with his usual affability. 'Keeping me busy today, gentlemen, aren't you? Two police cases in one day.'

'We're not sure yet if Muriel Galloway is a police case,' said Sloan cautiously. 'There's a *post mortem* because there are certain allegations that she died as a result of a drug trial.'

'So do most patients, Sloan,' said Dabbe cheerfully.

'I'm not sure, Doctor, that I—'

'You could say, Sloan, that everyone who dies

while they've been taking medication has been taking part in a drug trial.'

'Really, Doctor?'

'Well,' said Dabbe mischievously, 'the drugs have been tried, haven't they, and not worked.'

'Tried and failed, you mean?' Crosby looked interested at last.

'Right,' said the doctor.

'Or trial and error.' The constable caught the pathologist's drift more quickly than usual.

'Hit and miss often describes it better.' Dr Dabbe reached for his green operating gown.

Sloan was not disposed to argue with him. After all, the pathologist was in a better position to know that than anyone else.

'Otherwise known', continued the pathologist robustly, 'as "treating empirically".'

'What is being alleged in the case of Muriel Galloway, Doctor,' he said, 'is that her death was hastened by her taking part in what I am informed is called the Cardigan Protocol and perhaps – ' he coughed, 'it is not yet known if this was so – the drug that is being tested in that Protocol.'

'Ha!' said the pathologist, looking alert. 'Nice point, that, Sloan. And who may I ask, does know? Now that Meggie's dead, too, I mean.'

'It is believed', said Sloan carefully, 'that Dr Meggie did not know.'

'Ah, a double-blind trial. That's as it should be,

of course,' said Dabbe. 'So who does know?'

'I understand', said Sloan, 'that the pharmaceutical chemists, Gilroy's, over at Staple St James, have a list of those numbered bottles of tablets which contained the substance code-named Cardigan—'

'Which may or may not have been dangerous,' mused Dabbe, putting on a green surgical cap.

'—and those numbered bottles with tablets which appeared identical and which contained an inert substance.'

Dr Dabbe stroked his chin. 'And presumably poor old Meggie had a list of patients and the numbers on the bottles they have been given—'

'Yes, Doctor,' said Sloan steadily.

'Without knowing t'other from which?' said Crosby, who didn't like *post mortems* and was never in a hurry for them to get started.

'Right. And ne'er the twain set of matching numbers shall meet,' continued Dabbe, 'until the trial's well and truly over, I take it.'

'So I am told, Doctor.' Sloan cleared his throat and added, 'As a matter of interest, Gilroy's have their set of numbers and we – that is, the police – are holding Dr Meggie's figures for the – er – time being.'

Dr Dabbe cocked an eyebrow.

'Found in his car,' said Sloan succinctly. 'On the seat beside him. The Scenes of Crime people are still there. We'll get the body here for you as soon as we can, Doctor.'

'Alas, poor Meggie,' said Dr Dabbe.

'Quite so,' said Sloan.'

The pathologist became suddenly brisk. 'Right, let's look to the lady then—'

It was the best part of an hour before Dr Dabbe straightened up and pulled off his surgical gloves. 'Left ventricular failure, Sloan, and myocardial degeneration.'

'Natural causes—' That, thought Sloan, mindful of another appointment, would at least help him in dealing with Gordon Galloway.

'No doubt about it,' said the pathologist easily. 'She'd had a new hip and she'd had her tonsils and adenoids removed when a child but that's about it. Just what you'd expect in a woman of her age with her history.'

'No sign of any test drugs?'

'No sign of them having killed her,' qualified Dabbe, 'but I'll be reporting on the sections and specimens I've taken. There's certainly nothing macroscopic—'

'Macro—' Detective Constable Crosby was having his usual trouble with his notes.

'Opposite of microscopic, old chap. Means what you can see with the naked eye.'

The notes that Detective Inspector Sloan was making were mental ones. And he already suspected that there was more to this situation than met the eye, naked or otherwise.

'You're late back, Sloan,' barked Leeyes, when the two policemen returned to the police station at Berebury.

'Yes, sir,' agreed Sloan. That writer – George Bernard Shaw, he thought it had been – who had said, 'I never apologize' could not in the nature of things have ever met Superintendent Leeyes but his advice still held good.

'That son of the woman who died—'

'Gordon Galloway?' divined Sloan.

'Him. He's been waiting for you.'

'Yes, sir.'

'For a long time.'

'Yes, sir.'

'And he's pretty cross.'

For once the superintendent was not exaggerating. Gordon Galloway was very cross indeed and made it clear he was not used to being kept waiting.

'I'm sure I don't know what I pay my rates and taxes for, Inspector,' he began, every inch the busy man.

'No, sir.' Sloan resisted the temptation to refer him to the Town Hall for an answer to that question.

'Especially when something like this happens, Inspector. It's an outrage.'

'Yes, sir.' Of the four humours of mankind, there was no doubt which one fitted this short, portly man. It was choler.

'I tell you, Inspector, it's absolutely disgraceful. There's no other way of describing it. Disgraceful. The very day my mother died, too, and while she was being experimented on.'

'The pathologist', began Sloan, 'has—' but he got no further.

'First, I find my poor mother being used as a human guinea-pig on her last few days on earth—'

'I am informed, sir, that—'

'And then when we get home from the hospital I find the ultimate insult.'

'Where did you say, sir?'

'At home.'

'At home?' Sloan reached for his notebook. This was different.

'While my wife and I are over at the hospital making – er – the arrangements about my late mother, what happens?'

'What?' demanded Sloan crisply. He wouldn't want to be Gordon Galloway's secretary. That was one thing he was certain about.

'On my garage door,' said Galloway.

'What was on your garage door?' On second thoughts, he wouldn't want to work for Gordon Galloway in any capacity.

'This . . . . graffiti. Quite unspeakable.'

'What did it say?' asked Sloan. There was after all graffiti and graffiti. And probably a generation gap between Gordon Galloway and whoever put it there.

'Someone had written "No experiments on animals" all over my garage doors.'

'Anything else?' asked Sloan quickly.

'It called me . . .' said Galloway, turning a nasty shade of puce, 'Me! A medical collaborator.'

Chapter Ten

Treat persons who profess to be able to cure disease as you would fortune-tellers.

'So?' said Superintendent Leeye.

'So I've sent Crosby back to the hospital,' said Sloan, 'to ask Dr Chomel whether she was paged or made a telephone call about Muriel Galloway while she was stitching up Darren Clements, and within his hearing.'

Leeyes grunted. 'It won't only be him. You'll have to look out for the rest of his mob.'

'We're doing that—'

'Ten to one you'll find any one of a dozen of 'em could have written on Gordon Galloway's garage door.' He sniffed. 'If they can write, that is.'

'And sir,' Detective Inspector Sloan turned to something else, 'I think we are going to find that the Coroner is going to request a *post mortem* on Abel Granger of Willow End Farm.'

'You do, do you?' growled Leeyes. 'And are you

going to tell me why or wait until I work it out for myself?'

'He was on Dr Meggie's Cardigan Protocol, too,' said Sloan.

'I see. And because he's died, too, you think—'

'No, sir. It's not me. It's Dr Angus Browne. He says he won't sign the death certificate. Not since he's heard about Dr Meggie.'

'Hrrrmph.' The superintendent blew out his cheeks.

'Crosby didn't get any joy out of the switchboard operator at St Ninian's Hospital either. All she will say is that she was rung up early and asked to tell his underling that Dr Meggie wouldn't be in.'

'Not a lot of help, that, Sloan.'

'No, sir.' Sloan glanced down at his notebook. 'And as far as we can ascertain the last person that Dr Meggie would seem to have spoken to as he left the hospital yesterday evening is an artist—'

'An artist?' The superintendent's bushy eyebrows went up upon the instant.

'—who is working on a mural in the front entrance hall.'

'They didn't used to have artists—'

'Something, sir, to do with some scheme for brightening up older hospitals with – er – artistic efforts.'

'So what's this artist painting, then?' demanded Leeyes truculently.

'Actually, sir, this morning he's been working on some mice—'

'Mice!'

'Mice.' What they could have done with, decided Sloan, was Bruce Bairnsfather's Old Bill. 'Laboratory mice.'

'I don't know what the world is—'

'Adrian Gomm, that's the name of the artist, sir,' hurried on Sloan, 'says he's bringing the mice in because he thinks they're part of medicine, too.' Sloan still felt that Old Bill would have done it much better.

'Part of medicine?' snorted Leeyes.

'Yes, sir,' said Sloan, resisting a strong temptation to add 'Eye of newt, and toe of frog, Wool of bat, and tongue of dog' himself.

'I've heard of dormice for whooping cough,' said Leeyes, 'but surely we've come further than that by now? Why should mice come into the picture—'

'Because he says they're sufferers in the cause of medicine, too, sir.' Sloan's own first exchange with Adrian Gomm had also been quite combative. 'He thinks his mural should represent both the good and the bad in modern medicine.'

'If you ask me, Sloan,' countered Leeyes swiftly, 'he'll have his work cut out to do that.'

'The whole mural, you see, sir, is meant to be allegorical—' And he, Sloan, was meant to be enquiring into the deaths of Muriel Galloway and Paul

Meggie and quite possibly old Abel Granger as well. But he didn't say so: he had his pension to think of.

'I suppose that's something, Sloan,' grunted Leeyes. 'At least it's better than having open-heart surgery on view.' He stopped and glared at his subordinate. 'Or has he got that in as well?'

'Not yet,' said Sloan cautiously. 'What he has got is the bad on the left and the good on the right – that's traditional, he says, just like the theatre stage.'

'It may be traditional in art,' Leeyes said flatly, 'but let me remind you, Sloan, that down here at the police station the bad is all around us.'

'Yes, sir.' As Sloan understood it, that was the miasma theory of crime writ large. He probably felt the same way about medicine. 'As I was saying, sir,' – Sloan hoped that that point was being taken too but doubted it – 'the artist says he talked to Dr Meggie as he left the hospital last evening and he seemed quite cheerful then.'

'Whereabouts on the mural is he putting the mice?' asked Leeyes.

'In the middle, sir.'

'They piebald or something?'

'No, sir. White.'

'Can't he make up his mind which side to put them on, then?'

'It's not that, sir,' Detective Inspector Sloan took a deep breath and said, 'Adrian Gomm says he's put the mice in the middle because they're both a good and a bad component of research.'

'Tell me, Sloan,' said Leeyes, 'what is Detective Constable Crosby making of all this?'

'Not a lot,' said Detective Inspector Sloan truthfully.

Dr Angus Browne of Larking might have hedged about when talking to the family of his patient at Willow End Farm but he had done no such thing when he had been interviewed by the police in his own consulting room.

'No, Inspector, I was not called to see Abel Granger during last night, nor did I send for Dr Meggie until later in the day. The first message I had was sent here by the family to my surgery round about nine o'clock.'

'And what was the message?' asked Sloan. He was beginning to get very interested in every single message sent and received this morning.

'That old Abel had had a bad night and would I make him one of my first calls that morning.'

'And did you?' enquired Detective Constable Crosby, looking up. The family doctors he himself had so far encountered hadn't ever seemed as biddable as that.

'Aye.' Browne nodded. 'I'd been going to see him

today anyway. The man was going downhill pretty fast.'

'This message,' said Sloan. 'Do you know who rang you?'

'It would have been the daughter,' said the general practitioner confidently. 'Mrs Granger would no' have left him and the boys would have been out on the farm.'

Detective Inspector Sloan made a note to check that. 'And you confirm not only that you weren't sent for before then but that nor did you telephone Dr Meggie at five o'clock this morning to ask him to visit your patient.'

'I do.' He grimaced. 'I'd no' be asking a busy man like Meggie to get up in the middle of the night to see a hopeless case. After all he'd seen him in his out-patient clinic at the hospital weeks ago and said then that there was nothing to be done.'

'Except the Cardigan Protocol,' Sloan reminded him.

'Och, well, that was just a long shot that might have done some good.'

'But no harm?'

'Do you no' understand what I'm saying, Inspector?' Angus Browne drummed his fingers on his desk. 'I'm telling you the man was beyond aid. There was nothing to be lost in trying him on yon Protocol of Meggie's. Nothing at all. But that doesn't mean I'm prepared to sign something saying it had nothing to do with his dying. Not until I know it hadn't.'

Sloan switched direction before Crosby started taking an interest in the ethics of this. 'You say, Doctor, that you wouldn't have sent for Dr Meggie at five o'clock in the morning to see a hopeless case.'

'Aye, that's so.'

'But if you had,' asked Sloan, 'would he have come?'

'Of course,' responded Browne promptly. 'That's quite different.'

Sloan sighed. He doubted if he would ever master the niceties of medical interactions. Whilst there was obviously a fine balance on the general practitioner's part between deciding whether or not to send for the consultant, there was no such distinction when it came to his coming if sent for.

'You sent for him all right later in the morning, though,' said Crosby, pleased with himself at spotting an illogicality.

'Aye, but that wasn't for the patient,' said the doctor crisply.

'No?'

'That was for the relatives.'

'Ah—'

'And me,' said Angus Browne.

'You, Doctor?' said Sloan, surprised.

'Just in case they started feeling their father should have had more care and attention and wanted to take it up with me afterwards, you understand.' He grimaced. 'Some families get funny that way.'

'I see.' Sloan understood all right. They had that sort of trouble down at the police station, too. From people like Gordon Galloway.

'Not the mother,' said Browne. 'She knew the score all along. Besides, she's a sensible body. No, it's the younger boy there—'

'Christopher Granger . . . the one who found Dr Meggie?'

'Him.' Browne shot Sloan a keen look. 'He's a bit of an altruist and all that sort of thing?'

'What sort of thing exactly?' asked Sloan. It was a sad commentary on today's civilization that policemen had to be wary of altruists, but Sloan had found that when it came to the crunch they kicked as hard as the next man. And in much the same places.

Angus Browne stroked his chin. 'He had a bust-up with the local hunt last year.'

'Did he, indeed,' murmured Sloan.

'Persuaded his father not to let them on their land. Mind you, by then old Abel wasn't really up to arguing. Then Christopher started working on his brother to turn the farm over to organic production. The next thing was humane farming—'

Detective Constable Crosby suddenly sat up and started to take notice. 'That's when this little piggy doesn't go to market after all, isn't it?'

'You could put it like that,' said the general practitioner blandly, giving the constable a distinctly professional look. 'If you had a mind to.'

Dr Roger Byville pulled his car into Gilroy's Pharmaceuticals at Staple St James and walked in his usual measured way across the ample courtyard built in palmier days for carriages. He was at once ushered into the office of the Chief Chemist.

'Roger!' George Gledhill was on his feet the moment Byville crossed the threshold, his expression very solemn and his tone muted. 'You've heard about Paul, of course. All about him, I mean.'

Dr Byville regarded him impassively. 'I have.'

'Well?'

'Well what?' countered Byville, who enjoyed the advantage of a medical training and was thus a past master at not being stampeded into immediate comment.

'What would he want to go and do a thing like that for?'

'I can't tell you.' Byville took a chair. 'But no doubt it will emerge in due course.'

'Emerge!' spluttered Gledhill. 'Good grief, man, how do you think that we're going to—'

'He may have left a letter,' said Byville with a calm that Gledhill found disconcerting.

'Oh . . .' Gledhill's voice trailed away. 'Of course.'

'In my experience suicides usually do.'

Gledhill subsided. 'Naturally, you know more about these things than I do.'

'Yes,' said Byville calmly. 'Actually, he may have left two letters. In the circumstances.'

'I don't understand.' Gledhill looked up. 'What do you mean?'

'Didn't you know? Paul, poor fellow, was in the classic suicide situation. Not that he hadn't asked for it.'

'I still don't understand,' insisted the chemist.

'He was caught between a rock and a hard place.'

'Cardigan and . . . what else?'

'I'm not talking about Cardigan,' said Byville vigorously. 'I'm talking about his domestic problems.'

'Oh.' Gledhill looked blank. 'I didn't know he had any.'

'There was, on the one hand,' Byville informed him in his usual detached way, 'a very designing woman and on the other hand an equally determined daughter.'

Gledhill's face registered a relief that was quite comical to see as he said, 'I didn't know about them. It's Cardigan I've been worried about.'

'What about it?' asked Byville bluntly.

'Whether there'd been any . . . you know.'

But Byville wouldn't help him with words. 'No, I don't know.'

'Scientists are human, too, remember,' said

Gledhill obliquely, although now he came to think of it he'd never seen any signs of humanity in Roger Byville.

'Oh, Meggie was human, all right.' Byville gave a short laugh. 'If you ask me that was half his trouble.'

George Gledhill shook his head. 'I didn't mean that. I've been wondering whether things were all right with the Cardigan Protocol—'

'Lack of rigorous scrutiny in his data?' suggested Byville in a tone Gledhill didn't relish.

'There's always a lot of pressure for results,' said Gledhill, conveniently overlooking the fact that some of that very same pressure was applied by Gilroy's Pharmaceuticals.

'Publish or perish,' agreed Byville. 'That's the name of the game.'

'Fictitious results have been known,' said Gledhill, 'and fictitious patients, come to that—'

'And fictitious substances,' Roger Byville pointed out unkindly.

'—and', said Gledhill bleakly, 'we haven't got Meggie's Cardigan results. The police have got them.'

'Ah, yes,' murmured Byville, as if reminded of something. 'Cardigan. And what substance did you say that was?'

'A compound of the alkaloid fagarine and—' The Chief Chemist's chin came up suddenly. 'No, I think we'll leave it there, Roger. Until we see Paul's results ourselves.'

Chapter Eleven

Do not try to live for ever. You will not succeed.

The atmosphere of a house in mourning takes on a quality all of its own and Detective Inspector Sloan was alert for all the genuine signs of this when he and Crosby went back to the home of the late Dr Paul Meggie. The stillness of recent bereavement was certainly evident there: Bunty Meggie appeared to have been sitting where they had left her, some empty tea cups the only visible indication of the passage of time since the two policemen had been there before.

She hadn't changed her clothes and she was letting the telephone ring and ring – and ring.

'There's no one I want to hear from,' she said when the bell started again.

'It might be important,' suggested Sloan.

'It might be her,' said the girl with deep animosity.

It was the only sign of animation that she displayed. There was otherwise a dullness about her tone which showed that the reality of the death of her father had sunk in. She answered their questions in a remote, disinterested way but without hesitation. Yes, she was an only child. There had been another baby – a boy – but he had been what her mother had euphemistically described as 'born sleeping'.

'My father had always wanted a son,' she added listlessly.

She was, she declared, quite certain that the handwriting on the note calling him to Willow End Farm was his and she found some other samples of his handwriting for the two policemen without difficulty.

Detective Inspector Sloan put them into his folder with great care while Crosby said with surprise, 'I can actually read it.'

'He wrote very clearly,' she said gravely, 'for a doctor.'

'I wonder, miss,' said Sloan, 'if you would mind giving me an outline of your movements this morning after you heard your father's car leave?'

'I went back to sleep for a little while but I'd set my alarm for quite early because my partner and I—'

'Your partner, miss?' interposed Sloan. Now there was a word with a new meaning.

She flushed and said gauchely, 'My golf partner—'

'Ah—'

'She and I were due to play in the first foursome off the tee this morning.' She paused and pushed her hair back. 'It's funny how long ago this morning seems.'

'Yes, miss.' Time as a perception and time as a dimension were two separate things. Sloan knew this because it had been a proposition that Superintendent Leeyes had had to debate in one of his Adult Education Classes: and he had sought the views of every serving officer in 'F' Division. That had been before he had been asked to leave the class over a misunderstanding about Galileo, velocity and the Leaning Tower of Pisa. 'Did you have any breakfast?'

'I had a very good breakfast,' she said, 'because I knew that I'd need it. You can't play a full round at Kinnisport on an empty stomach. It's a tough course.'

'No, miss, I'm sure. Tell me, did your father have anything to eat before he went out?'

She shook her head. 'I'm sure he didn't. For one thing, Inspector, if someone wanted him at five o'clock in the morning they wanted him pretty badly—'

Detective Inspector Sloan was in complete agreement with her there. He was beginning to realize someone had wanted Dr Paul Meggie very badly indeed but not, he now thought, to give a medical opinion. 'And for another thing, miss?'

'He'd have left the washing up,' she said simply. 'He always did.'

For the second time that day, Detective Inspector Sloan and Detective Constable Crosby were attending a *post-mortem* examination. And while it would have been true to say that in between times they had both grabbed some food, Sloan for one wasn't sure that he had digested his.

Dr Dabbe welcomed them with unimpaired courtesy. 'Or should I be saying, "Once more into the breach, dear friends, once more"?' he said, leading the way into the mortuary.

Even though it was the speech that every schoolboy learned by heart, all Sloan could call to mind at this moment was something melancholy which went with it about 'our English dead'. He hoped he wasn't going to have to add Abel Granger to the list of today's *post mortems*. Berebury was, after all, not Harfleur.

The laboratory attendant eased back the sheet from the face of the late Paul Meggie and Detective Inspector Sloan took his second look at the man. While Dr Dabbe regarded the body of his former colleague with apparent equanimity, Sloan considered what he saw before him with a professional detachment. He had never seen Paul Meggie in life. Even in death, though, he could see that the man must have been very personable. His features had a quite distinguished cast to them, while his little grey-ing moustache was neatly trimmed and his figure still that of an active man.

'How good a doctor was he?' Sloan was more than a little reminded by Paul Meggie's face of the copy of the death mask of Agamemnon which had adorned the upper corridor of his school. After all, they couldn't all be as bad doctors as Dangerous Dan McGrew or there wouldn't be anyone left alive in Calleshire.

'Meggie was no fool,' Dr Dabbe said promptly. 'He'd got that rare commodity called clinical acumen. Not enough of it about these days. Good judgement is very important in a physician.'

Sloan nodded. They had policemen in the Force with acumen – and policemen without it. And good judgement couldn't be taught: that was something he'd never believed but he had learned it the hard way.

'Good clinicians', pronounced Dabbe, 'are a much under-rated commodity in these mechanized days, I can tell you, gentlemen.'

'Mechanized?' Crosby sat up. 'Medicine?'

Dabbe waved a hand airily. 'Scans, X-rays, patho-logy, computers and so forth but I can assure you that under all those trimmings and his showmanship

Meggie was a really good doctor. He didn't', said Dabbe, paying the ultimate medical tribute by one doctor to another, 'miss much.'

'Which you would have found even if he didn't?' said Sloan. There was no fresh carnation in Paul Meggie's buttonhole now but Sloan fancied Dr Dabbe's little encomium would have pleased the man more.

'True. And for my sort of pathology,' said Dabbe ironically, 'you can read "hindsight".' He suffered himself to be eased into his gown by his assistant and prepared to advance on the subject.

Detective Constable Crosby, ever anxious to postpone the first incision, asked the pathologist what it was like cutting up someone you knew.

Dabbe shot the constable a penetrating look. 'It's no different from examining anyone else,' he said chillingly. 'You can't afford to have feelings in medicine.'

Sloan, who had found the same thing applied to policing, opened his mouth to say just that but Crosby, greatly daring, forestalled him.

'There must be something, Doctor,' he persisted, 'that upsets you.'

'Crosby!' Sloan stiffened. 'I'm very sorry, Doctor,' he apologized rigidly, 'that my constable should have allowed his curiosity to get the better of him—' Crosby he would deal with later. In the privacy of the police station.

'No, no, Sloan,' said Dabbe, stooping over the body of the dead man and beginning his external examination. 'It's a good question. The boy's quite right. We've all got an Achilles' heel. Mine, I don't mind telling you, is cars.'

'Cars, Doctor?' echoed Sloan.

'Don't like seeing crashed cars,' admitted Dabbe, by far and away the fastest living driver in Calleshire. 'A good car is a beautiful thing. Sends a shiver down my spine when I see a badly damaged one.'

'What I don't like is—' began Crosby.

'And as for seeing them upside down in the ditch—' The pathologist shuddered and lowered his head again. 'I think it's downright obscene.'

It hadn't occurred to Sloan that there might be an intimate side to a car, too.

It seemed only a moment or two before the pathologist straightened up and said in his usual tones, 'See the October flush on his face? That spells carbon monoxide poisoning to me.'

'Ah . . .' Sloan knew all about the October flush: birds' nests in the chimney in the summer, gas fires in the chimney in the autumn. Result: carbon monoxide poisoning in the human. 'I am told he was on the – er – horns of a family dilemma.'

The pathologist wasn't listening. He was once again bending over the *post-mortem* table but now his whole manner had changed. He reached for a magnifying glass and resumed his scrutiny of Paul Meggie's face. It was the deceased's mouth and lips that were engaging his attention.

Somehow the atmosphere of the mortuary changed to match Dr Dabbe's demeanour. The stillness of his concentration was pretty nearly palpable. Sloan almost held his breath in sympathy. If Crosby said so much as a word now, he, Sloan, would personally take him apart.

At long last Dr Dabbe put the magnifying glass down and spoke. 'I can't be absolutely sure, Sloan, but I think that what I am looking at are some slight burn marks around the mouth?'

'Burn marks?' Burn marks brought in a new dimension. Sloan said, 'But what about the carbon monoxide, Doctor? There was a tube from the exhaust into the car. I saw it.'

Dr Dabbe looked unusually grim. 'I think we are going to find that the burn marks preceded the carbon monoxide poisoning.'

'But—'

'In fact, Sloan, I think we might postulate that they facilitated it.'

Detective Inspector Sloan was not a man to stand on ceremony. 'I'm sorry, Doctor, but I just don't understand.'

'I'm not at all sure that I do,' said Dabbe, looking down at the body of a man he knew, 'but what I think we are looking at here might be second-degree burns.'

'Burn marks?' echoed Superintendent Leeyes. 'What exactly are you trying to tell me, Sloan?'

'The pathologist', quoted Detective Inspector Sloan, 'is of the considered opinion that some substance as yet unidentified was applied to or made contact with in some other way—'

'And what is that supposed to mean?' interrupted Leeyes truculently.

'Sprayed,' said Sloan cogently.

Leeyes sniffed. 'Go on.'

'Made contact with the area round the deceased's mouth and nose immediately prior to his death.'

'What he's saying then, Sloan, is that this—'

'He suggests' – Sloan turned over a page of his notes – 'that the application of this substance – liquid or gaseous, he doesn't know which yet – might have been made with a view to rendering the deceased incapable of action while the carbon monoxide gas from the car exhaust took effect.'

'He does, does he? And', barked Leeyes, 'does he have any happy thoughts on what this substance might have been?'

'Two possibilities that he put forward', responded Sloan sturdily, 'are a riot-control agent or chloroform.'

'So,' said Superintendent Leeyes ineluctably, 'it's not suicide.'

'No, sir.' That much had been apparent to the detective inspector in that Temple of Truth, the *post-mortem* laboratory.

'Or accident,' concluded Leeyes aloud, 'or natural causes—'

'No, sir. In fact, Dr Dabbe says the deceased was particularly healthy for his age.'

Leeyes growled, 'That leaves murder—'

'Very probably, sir.'

'I don't like it.'

'No, sir.' Neither did Sloan, his free weekend irretrievably lost now. Reminded by this, he said, 'There's something about this weekend, sir.'

'What's that?'

Sloan coughed. 'Dr Dabbe managed to convey to us without, of course, being in any way medically unprofessional or unethical, sir, that—'

Superintendent Leeyes conveyed without any difficulty at all what he thought about self-serving medical ethics.

'Quite so, sir,' responded Sloan. 'You see, these burn marks are absolutely minimal—'

'Well?'

'If, sir, Paul Meggie's body hadn't been found until later - say this evening or tomorrow - which, seeing it was on a side track, was quite on the cards—'

'Get on with it, Sloan.'

'Yes, sir. Or if Dr Dabbe had felt he shouldn't be doing the *post-mortem* examination on account of his knowing Dr Meggie personally—'

'I shouldn't have thought he was one to be squeamish,' growled Leeyes. 'I reckon he's as cold-blooded as they come.'

Sloan let this pass and carried on, 'Then his stand-in, who's from the other side of Calleshire, would have had to do the *post mortem*—'

'So?'

Sloan said delicately, 'I understand this other chap's been known to miss small things—'

'Ah, I see. He's the Dangerous Dan McGrew of the pathological world, is he!' snorted Leeyes. 'Is that what you're trying to say?'

'Sort of, sir,' Sloan said, adding, 'Of course, it won't be so dangerous when it's a pathologist operating, not a surgeon.'

'Nonsense,' said Leeyes roundly. 'The law is much more important, Sloan, than an individual life. Don't you realize that the police are guardians of the social fabric of this country? And if murder goes unrecognized as murder, then where are we?'

'It would have been this man who would have examined the deceased,' said Sloan steadily.

'Why wouldn't Dr Dabbe have been available then?'

'He's racing his Westerly at the Kinnisport Regatta all weekend.'

'And who knew that?'

'Everyone who read yesterday's local newspaper,' said Detective Inspector Sloan, a touch of melancholy in his voice. 'He was last year's winner and the paper did a feature on him.'

Chapter Twelve

It is always safer to operate.

In purely chronological terms Martin Friar was barely a year older than Dilys Chomel. Medically speaking, though, he felt he was already well on his way to early middle age.

Nevertheless even he, more experienced as he was, did not feel he could cope without some support with the imminent death on Lorkyn Ward of a young man. He had telephoned the Women's Medical Ward at Berebury Hospital – and got Dilys Chomel instead of Dr Byville.

'I'm afraid he's gone over to Gilroy's,' said Dilys. 'Is it urgent?' Three months ago she would have asked if it was important. Now only the urgent mattered: everything else in her day had to be subordinated to that which would not wait.

'It's this spleen of Dr Byville's we shipped over here the other day to be nearer his family. Remember?'

'I remember.' Dilys Chomel had not forgotten only because she had been grateful at the time to have one fewer very ill patient to look after.

'He's not going to do,' said Martin Friar who had also picked up the correct lingo, doctor to doctor. 'And I've already', he added ruefully, 'got it in the neck anyway for agreeing to take him.'

Dilys gave a little shiver which she was glad he couldn't see. 'We've got a woman here who's just the same. She's going downhill all the time.'

'My chap's spleen was compromised by chemo-therapy—'

'This woman was in a road smash.'

'What's yours on?'

Dilys detailed a list of drugs.

'Mine, too,' he said gloomily. 'He's having exactly the same. Actually there's a woman in the female ward here doing better on something different but old Byville won't let me put my chap on it too. He said changing therapeutic horses in midstream could be clinically dangerous.'

'It can't be more dangerous than dying, surely,' objected Dilys.

'Don't you believe it,' said Friar with feeling. He'd already learned that in hospital there were a great many things for a doctor worse than a patient dying. Some of them were worse for the patient, too.

'Dr Byville hasn't suggested prescribing anything different for the woman here,' said Dilys Chomel, 'so, whatever it is, it can't be all that good.' She paused before saying tentatively, 'You've heard about Dr Meggie, I'm sure?' They didn't have what she supposed she should call 'active suicide' in her home country and she didn't like to put the phrase into words.

'I have indeed. I must say I was surprised,' said Martin Friar judiciously. 'He didn't ever strike me as that type at all.'

'Nor me,' said Dilys humbly. 'He always seemed to me to be on top of everything.' She herself was very conscious of not being on top of a lot of things these days.

'Always.'

'I suppose something was too much for him after all.' If someone committed an offence against society where Dilys Chomel came from they were expected just to go home and die. Of inanition, usually; absolution was unheard of.

'You never know with these things,' said Friar sagaciously.

'Perhaps he was a bit of a dark horse,' suggested Dilys.

'Doggish, more like,' said Martin Friar. 'I hear there's a *femme fatale* in the woodwork.' Friar, who was not yet thirty, still thought the idea of late-middle-aged marriage faintly risible.

'What we would call an old goat,' said Dilys surprisingly.

'Perhaps.' He changed his tone. 'Or it could be something else, something quite different.'

'What's that?'

'We've already had the police here,' he said, 'asking which patients had been entered for the Cardigan Protocol. I should think they'll be with you soon.'

She ventured a question. 'What do you think was wrong with Cardigan?'

'Something,' he said evasively, 'but don't ask me what.'

The police weren't on their way to Berebury Hospital. They were at Gilroy's Pharmaceuticals at Staple St James. With some difficulty Sloan had persuaded Crosby that the wide sweep of the carriage drive was not a place for exhibition motoring. He directed him instead to the stables entrance. Discreet as their arrival had therefore been it clearly threw the Chief Chemist and his deputy.

'Just one or two more questions, gentlemen,' said Sloan civilly.

George Gledhill regarded him warily. 'Such as?'

'Was Paul Meggie the only doctor testing Cardigan for you?'

'Yes and no,' hedged Gledhill.

'And what does that mean?' There was, after all, no such 'yes and no' about Paul Meggie's being dead.

'He was the only one, Inspector, who was what you might describe as being presently actively engaged on round two of Cardigan,' said Gledhill.

'Suppose', invited Sloan, 'you tell me about round one.' From where he was sitting he could just see the top of the large, old conservatory where the monkeys lived in semi-tropical temperatures. 'Before we go on to round two,' he added.

'That was last year.' George Gledhill did not look a happy man. 'We did the usual trials up and down the country – a proper statistical and demographic spread—'

'Don't forget the sociological one, too,' put in Mike Itchen, who had been following their exchange very closely.

'In my experience nobody ever forgets the sociological,' said Sloan balefully.

'No,' said Gledhill. 'Well, the results from round one were what you might call distinctly equivocal.'

'They didn't either prove or disprove the efficacy of the compound,' translated Itchen.

'So?'

'So, Inspector,' said Gledhill, 'Mike here designed what you might call a more elegant second round.'

'It was more clinically and chemically discriminating,' said Itchen modestly.

'And', the Chief Chemist carried on more confidently, 'Paul Meggie – because he was local and interested – was doing a trial run with a pilot test of this.'

Detective Inspector Sloan said, 'Are you telling me that Dr Meggie was the only doctor running this particular test?'

The temperature in the Chief Chemist's room was already considerably lower than that in the conservatory. It fell still further as he said, 'I'm afraid so, gentlemen.'

'And when, may I ask,' said Sloan, although he thought he might already know, 'was Dr Meggie due to hand over to you the results of the trial run of this elegant and clinically and chemically more discriminating pilot test?'

'Lunchtime today,' said Gledhill hollowly.

'Which means,' spelled out Crosby, who appeared to have been doing nothing but look out of the window, 'does it, that now nobody knows? By the way, what's that funny hedge thing out there?'

'A maze,' said Gledhill distractedly. 'No, it doesn't mean that nobody knows the results. It means that nobody knows them until we see them and put them together with the names in our records.'

'And then we'll know', said Mike Itchen, 'whether the trial run worked.'

'If, that is,' said Gledhill, putting in a caveat, 'Dr Meggie actually completed them before his death.'

'There is also the possibility,' remarked Sloan in a detached way, 'the purely theoretical possibility, of course, that Dr Meggie completed his records and did not like the results.'

Detective Constable Crosby looked round the room and said brightly, 'Or that he had completed his records and there was someone else who didn't like them.'

'Well?' demanded Superintendent Leeyes. The superintendent's weekend off-duty was sacrosanct even if no one else's was and he was anxious to be gone. 'You're making progress, I hope, Sloan.'

'We've begun to establish a number of parameters,' said Sloan, generously implying that Crosby had been helpful in this exercise. 'And also that Gilroy's keep some personal-protection devices on their premises in the form of propellant sprays.'

'What are they afraid of?' enquired Leeyes with interest. 'Mice or men?'

At Gilroy's Pharmaceuticals he had been told that their chief anxiety when attacked by the animal liberationists was not letting the fruit flies escape since it seemed that a nuclear fast-breeder reactor had nothing on *Drosophila bifurca* for speedy reproduction. Which, apparently, was very helpful in research.

Sloan decided against going into this with the superintendent and said instead that he and Crosby had then gone over to the Kinnisport Golf Club.

'Links,' said Leeyes.

'Pardon, sir?'

'A seaside golf course typified by sand, turf and coarse grass of the kind on which the game of golf was originally played,' his superior officer informed him.

'Really, sir?'

'They're known as links, Sloan.'

Detective Inspector Sloan made a careful note. It was perfectly true to say that you learned something new every day. It was just that he didn't usually learn it from the superintendent, that was all.

'They confirmed over there that Miss Bunty Meggie did take part in a golf competition all morning.' Sloan consulted his notebook. 'It was something called a four-ball medal round. Would that be right, sir?' Sloan was not a golfer and the superintendent was. That was why his weekends off-duty were so inviolable.

'What isn't right, Sloan, is that the ladies should be playing a four-ball medal round at all.' Leeyes snorted indignantly. 'Shouldn't be allowed, that's what I say.'

Sloan thought that he already knew by heart everything that the superintendent thought shouldn't be allowed. Here, obviously, was yet something else.

'Holds up everyone on the course behind them,'

said Leeyes, adding with his usual didactism, 'Their committee should put a stop to it at once—'

'According to the Ladies' Captain, sir, Miss Meggie arrived there at about seven forty-five, hitting her first shot off the tee on the stroke of eight. The ladies went out at five-minute intervals and the course was closed to everyone else until half-past nine—'

'What did I tell you, Sloan? It shouldn't be allowed.'

'Therefore,' Sloan ploughed on, 'Miss Meggie's movements are accounted for after the time it would have taken her to get to the golf cour– links from her house or wherever else she started from—'

'Ah!' Superintendent Leeyes pounced. 'Are you saying, Sloan, that she could have been the one—'

'Crosby is measuring the distance between Dr Meggie's house and the place where he was found now, sir.'

'And you, I take it, Sloan,' said Leeyes sourly, 'are making due allowance for Crosby's speed?'

'And he is also', said Sloan, 'establishing exactly how far it is from Willow End Farm to the Kinnisport Links to see if, at a speed unlikely to attract comment—'

'Talking of speed attracting comment, Sloan,' began Leeyes, 'let me tell you that Inspector Harpe tells me that Constable Crosby—'

'She could have done the distance in the time.'

Inspector Harpe was head of Traffic Division and not an admirer of Crosby's driving.

'You're talking about normal speeds now, aren't you?'

'Yes, sir.' Mention of the combination of speed, time and distance conjured up the spectre of Galileo again so Sloan added swiftly, 'I don't know if it's relevant sir, but the Ladies' Captain said that Bunty Meggie played to her handicap in this competition they were having there this morning.'

For some mysterious reason that did meet with his approval. 'Good, good, Sloan. Mind you, a four-ball medal round is so slow that you've got time to get into form.'

'Really, sir?' Bunty Meggie hadn't struck Sloan as the sort of woman to be put off her stroke very easily anyway. He amended this: the thought of her father's remarriage had certainly got to her.

He put the real question to Detective Constable Crosby when they met in the canteen a little later. 'The point was also raised, you may remember, Crosby, in the old nursery rhyme called "An Elegy on the Death of Cock Robin".' He hadn't himself realized when young the close links between nursery rhymes and crime.

'Bunty Meggie could have done the distance in the time, sir,' said Crosby, pulling out his notebook. 'From Larking to Kinnisport—'

'That was also a case of "Who'll be chief mourner?"; said Sloan, sinking a mug of hot tea.

'Although it's not a very good road until you get to—'

' "I, said the dove",' quoted Sloan. 'It was exactly who the dove was that mattered, Crosby.'

But he was talking to himself. Crosby had gone back for buns.

' "I mourn for my love",' declaimed Detective Inspector Sloan to the empty air. ' "I'll be chief mourner".'

'There's currant or jam,' said Crosby, plonking the buns down on their table.

'There's Hannah Glawari—' said Sloan.

Chapter Thirteen

As to the honour and conscience of doctors, they have as much as any other class of men, no more and no less.

Even in hospitals Saturdays are different from weekdays. Shirley Partridge never minded being on duty at the weekend. The pressure of incoming calls was less then and this left her free to chat to those coming and going in the entrance hall. Saturdays were different for Dr Marion Teal, too. The woman-hating Mr Maldonson had no need to make her late for her child-minder on Saturdays since her husband would be at home. This morning she had left the hospital at the right time without having to wait on his pleasure.

Saturdays were the same as any other day for Adrian Gomm, the artist. It was the state of the light that dictated his work, not the calendar, and today the light was good. He was halfway up his ladder when Dr Edwin Beaumont came in. The doctor paused as usual to observe the work in progress on the mural.

'Ah,' he said, recognizing some old medical symbolism, 'you've started on one of the serpents.'

'And not our old friend from the Garden of Eden either,' grinned Gomm. 'I put the Great Divide in yesterday.'

'The axis,' said Edwin Beaumont appreciatively.

'And I'll do the other serpent after this one.'

'Caduceus.'

'Light and dark, conscious and unconscious, male and female, beginning and end,' recited Gomm.

'Youth and age, summer and winter, past and future, death and life,' added Dr Beaumont. 'That reminds me. I'd better be getting along. I've someone to see on Barnesdale Ward.' He tapped on Shirley Partridge's glass cubicle window as he went by. 'Any messages for me?'

But there were no messages awaiting him and he went on his way towards the rickety old lift, and then, later, to the clinic to which his private patients were admitted. He was walking down one of their quiet, carpeted corridors when he spotted a familiar figure ahead of him.

'Roger! There you are.' Beaumont quickened his pace until he caught up with him. 'I thought I might see you here. Is there any more news about Paul's death, do you know?'

Dr Byville paused on his way and shook his head.

'None that I've heard. I had poor Bunty on the phone for an age last night though.'

'She'll need to talk to somebody.'

'She wanted to be told all about the wretched Cardigan Protocol. Paul hadn't said a thing about it to her, naturally.'

'Do you think it was that which drove him to it?'

'I couldn't say,' said Byville, shrugging his shoulders.

'He was a bit wrapped up in it.'

'I said to Bunty that her father was the only person who could have told her anything really important about it. If there was anything to tell. Who knows?'

Dr Edwin Beaumont stroked his chin in the gesture of thought. It was a movement that always went down well with his patients, who were left with the impression that he was thinking about them. 'Do you think there's anything in Cardigan?'

'I don't see how we can possibly tell at this stage, can we?'

'Suppose not,' said Beaumont peaceably. 'All the same, it's all a great pity.'

'Of course it's a great pity,' said Byville with feeling. 'Quite apart from anything else, Paul had a lot more work and research in him. And now we're going to be left short-handed for God knows how long.'

'It'll take them an age to get a *locum tenens*,'

agreed Beaumont, no friend of the administration at any time, 'let alone appoint someone else.'

'They've already been talking about re-arranging our duties,' said Byville. 'And that, as we both know very well, means more work. A lot more work.'

'There's the Senior Registrar, Friar.'

'Much good he is,' said Byville contemptuously. 'He had me out early this morning because that spleen I showed you on Lorkyn was dying. I'd told him yesterday that the man hadn't a hope in hell.' He sniffed. 'These days I don't expect the public to understand that we can't save everyone but I did think a senior registrar would have worked it out by now.'

'I hear', said the other doctor, 'that the *p.m.* on Angus Browne's patient over at Larking – you know, the one on whose farm Paul was – er – found – was absolutely straightforward even though he was on the Cardigan Protocol, too.'

'How do we know?' he demanded irritably. 'How does anyone know who's on what in a double-blind trial?'

'Afterwards, Roger. They can always tell afterwards.'

'Not when the police have one set of records and the drug people the other, they can't,' responded Byville with vigour. He gave an unamused bark of laughter. 'Didn't you know they've taken Paul's records into protective custody? Gledhill over at Gilroy's is fit to be tied.'

'Do we know what Cardigan comprises?'

'It's a compound of fagarine and some other substance, the name of which', he added acidly, 'Gilroy's are not prepared to disclose at this juncture.'

'Fagarine,' mused Edwin Beaumont. 'Now that, I agree, is something that could bear being looked at again.' He halted in his tracks, deep in thought. 'It would be very interesting to administer fagarine with a catalyst and measure the reaction. More interesting still, of course,' he went on, suddenly alert, 'would be to put it with a synergist.'

'If you ask me,' – Roger Byville lowered his voice, – 'the synergic agent in all of this is a widow called Mrs Hannah Glawari. Not only bringing about change but being changed by it herself—'

'True synergy,' murmured Beaumont as the sister in charge of the clinic bore down upon them both. 'I must remember to look up fagarine. It's an alkaloid, I think—'

Saturdays were different from weekdays at the police station, too. This was principally because Superintendent Leeyes seldom came in then. Detective Inspector Sloan, sitting in his meagre office there, was grateful for this small mercy, although – Saturday or not – he realized that the early scented rose 'Celeste' was destined to be born unseen and waste its sweetness on his friend's deserted greenhouse air without him, and Crosby had, as usual, been late.

'Had any further thoughts since you went home last night?' Sloan asked him.

'I went off-duty, sir, when I went home,' Crosby reminded him reproachfully.

'Have you had any fresh thoughts this morning, then?' enquired Sloan with an elaborate politeness quite lost on the constable. 'Such as who it would be best to interview next?'

Crosby frowned prodigiously. 'Perhaps we should lean on Christopher Granger.'

'The farmer's son?'

'He found the body, didn't he?' said Crosby unanswerably. 'And so he would have had time to do what he wanted with it.'

'We could establish if he was out and about very early yesterday morning.' Sloan made a note. 'Although I dare say the rest of the family would have been too preoccupied nursing the old man to notice.'

'Christopher Granger could have guessed that Dr Meggie would know how very ill his father was.'

'True.'

'And all he had to do', persisted Crosby, 'was to tell him to take the left fork on the farm road and not the right.'

'And we don't know whether the deceased recognized the voice on the telephone, do we, since he's not alive to tell us.' Sloan made a note.

'Someone lured him to his doom,' said Crosby sepulchrally.

'Motive?' asked Sloan, since he himself had done some thinking overnight and, anyway, was supposed to be teaching the constable about criminal investigation.

'Perhaps he didn't like his poor old father being experimented on.' The lack of objectivity of this observation was underlined by Crosby's next remark. 'He struck me as being a bit of a wet.'

'Wets don't usually have the bottle to murder anyone,' said Sloan, reminding himself to explain to the constable some time what a field day any defence counsel would have with a police officer who couldn't distinguish between fact and opinion. 'Unless they're really pushed.'

'Christopher Granger's into one of these animal rights groups, too,' said Crosby darkly, 'and you never know what they'll do if they're pushed.'

To Detective Inspector Sloan there would always be one mystery that defeated him and that was the reason for man's inhumanity to man. And to his mind cruelty to animals came in the same category of utter and total inexplicability. As far as he was concerned as both a man and as a policeman both were quite inexcusable.

'Abel Granger's *post mortem* revealed nothing but heart failure,' he countered, feeling this was no moment for taking this up with the detective constable.

Crosby sniffed. 'That pathologist who's standing in for Dr Dabbe couldn't find a needle in a needle case.'

'And is that fact or opinion?'

'Didn't you know, sir? He's the one they use when one of Dangerous Dan's patients has gone and died on the operating table.'

Such cynicism about the medical profession in one so young didn't seem quite right. Sloan said, 'What about the stun gas, then?'

'Everyone's using it these days,' said the detective constable airily.

'Except us,' said Sloan with feeling. Incapacitant sprays were quicker by far than the mayor standing on the town hall steps reading the Riot Act to the mob. They worked better, too.

'Don't you remember, sir? Gilroy's had some stun gas stolen two attacks back. Theirs was a veterinary variety and they were trying to put the monkeys out of action so that they wouldn't escape—'

'And the animal rights activists alleged they were trying to get them and not the monkeys. I remember all right,' agreed Sloan bitterly. 'They tried to sue Gilroy's for common assault and it was a near thing with the Bench.'

'You never know with magistrates,' said Crosby profoundly.

'No,' said Sloan. Perhaps his own lessened faith in the magistrates was just a sign that he'd been a policeman too long. 'Tell me, do you have any other candidates for interview after Christopher Granger?'

'There's that Darren Clements and his little lot,' said Crosby promptly. 'I've never seen a man look more like a ferret myself. I reckon, sir, that he was after something at Gilroy's, all right.'

'Trouble?' suggested Sloan. He'd never known a trouble-seeker yet who didn't rationalize his goals and animal rights were as good as any.

'This Cardigan thing that keeps cropping up,' said Crosby. 'Perhaps there was something in it for him and his pals too.'

'As far as I can gather,' said Sloan mildly, 'all the trials for the Cardigan Protocol were being done on human beings.'

Crosby dismissed this with a wave of his hand. 'That pompous businessman whose old mother died yesterday—'

'Gordon Galloway.'

'He had something funny written on his walls.'

'Anti-animal research slogans.'

Crosby nodded. 'Well, I saw that young lady doctor with the hair, like you said, sir.'

'Dilys Chomel.'

'She did have a call about Muriel Galloway,' said

Crosby, 'within earshot of Darren Clements. She was stitching him up in Accident and Emergency when they sent for her from the ward because Mrs Galloway had died.'

Sloan stared out of the police station window for a long moment. There was a thread running through the tapestry of all the activity round about Dr Meggie's death that seemed, wherever they looked, always to be pulling their attention back to Cardigan – or was it to Gilroy's Pharmaceuticals?

'And someone, Crosby,' he said, 'don't forget, notified us that Muriel Galloway had been on Cardigan. A woman, switchboard thought.' Where did Muriel Galloway come into all this, even if her death had been what Dr Dabbe had been pleased to call natural? He didn't know yet but he would find out.

'Don't forget, sir, that it was a woman, too, who rang the Kinnisport Hospital switchboard about Dr Meggie not coming in yesterday morning,' said Crosby. 'That stuck-up telephonist there is sure about it. Mind you,' he sniffed, 'I reckon she'd have gone to the stake if it would have helped Dr Meggie. Proper heart throb he must have been.'

'Some people get like that about doctors,' said Sloan wisely. 'Don't ask me why. They never get crushes on policemen. Now, do you have anyone else in mind for questioning?'

'The doctor's daughter,' said Crosby without hesitation. 'Anyone could have got back to their house in Kinnisport from Willow End Farm, taken in the milk bottles or whatever and then got to the golf course in the ordinary way.'

'Links,' said Sloan unfairly.

'Links, then,' said Crosby, 'before eight o'clock.'

'And where would she have got the stun gas?'

'Personal-defence canister,' said Crosby. 'You can buy 'em anywhere you like on the Continent. Or, since her old man was a medico, perhaps he had some chloroform.' Suddenly Crosby contrived to look extremely worldly wise. 'And you're not going to ask me about motive, sir, are you?'

'No,' said Sloan. There had been too marked an absence of references by Bunty Meggie to 'O My Beloved Father' for that. 'And should we be talking to anyone else at all, do you think?'

'The Merry Widow,' said Crosby without hesitation.

'Any reason?'

'Sorry, sir. I meant to tell you. I had a word with Puckle, Puckle and Nunnery, like you said.'

'The deceased's solicitors?'

'That's right. They said that Dr Meggie had drawn up a will written in expectation of marriage.'

'Ah—'

'But not signed it.' He drew breath. 'Sir, she might not have known whether or not he'd signed it—'

'True.'

'And she could have had an assignation over at Willow End Farm with the deceased.'

'How would you account for the message by the bed?' enquired Sloan with interest.

'A blind,' said Crosby largely. 'Assignations have to be mysterious, don't they? And that address would fool the daughter.'

'And Mrs Glawari', mused Sloan, thinking aloud along quite different lines, 'could have known Paul Meggie had a very poorly patient at Willow End Farm at Larking because he could have told her.'

'Perhaps they always met there,' said Crosby. 'Romantic spot, down by the river and all that.'

There had been nothing romantic in Sloan's eyes at the scene that had met him by the little river at Willow End Farm. Nothing at all. Just a man dead in middle age, the good car and the expensive suiting mere artefacts to an untimely end. Sloan had to admit, though, that the little clearing in the willows beside the stream would have been a good place for a secret meeting.

'And her motive?' he asked.

'Dr Meggie could have told Mrs Glawari he wasn't going to marry her after all,' said Crosby. 'You know, sir, laid it on heavy that he couldn't leave his daughter on her own after all.'

'It's a thought, Crosby, especially with hell having no fury like a woman scorned.'

'I wouldn't know about that, sir, but I can't see

any Prince Charming coming for our Bunty,' said Crosby frankly. 'Not with those legs.'

'No.' Sloan had to concede that White Knights were likely to be thin on the ground as far as the muscular Miss Meggie was concerned.

'And I guess the other lady wouldn't have liked the daughter coming first.'

'Definitely not.' Sloan stood up to go. 'Puts a whole new meaning on the expression *femme fatale*, doesn't it, Crosby? Come on, let's go.'

Chapter Fourteen

What you want is comfort, reassurance, something to clutch at, be it but a straw. This the doctor brings you.

While Saturdays were admittedly not usually working days at Gilroy's Pharmaceuticals – except for those who monitored the animals – this particular Saturday morning found both George Gledhill and Mike Itchen at the firm at Staple St James. Detective Inspector Sloan had been assured that it would be no trouble – positively no trouble at all – to meet him there with their side of the Cardigan Protocol reference numbers.

'Have you got those figures from Dr Meggie's car all right?' Sloan asked Crosby as they approached the old mansion.

'Copies, like you said,' answered Crosby. 'Forensics are still playing with the real ones.'

Sloan grunted. He wasn't at all sure at this stage how they would be able to tell whether or not the figures had been dollied up. Or, if so, who by. But there were specialists enough in the Force who could work out anything. There were some financial frauds these days that were so clever that policemen had to go to business school to learn how to work them out. By comparison research results shouldn't be a problem.

'There's only Paul Meggie's fingerprints on them,' Crosby assured him.

'That's something, I suppose,' said Sloan in a world where very little else seemed straightforward.

'Oh, and one thumb print of his secretary's on the top page.' He screwed up his face in an effort of recollection. 'Forensics said to say there's no sign of any of the figures having been messed about with but they'll have another look to make sure.'

If Sloan knew Forensics they would have put it more elegantly – let alone more scientifically – than that. 'And you've found both Muriel Galloway and Abel Granger on the list?'

'Named with a number beside them.' Crosby patted the parcel under his arm. 'And some notes of how they were doing.'

'Badly,' said Sloan, since he wasn't a doctor and saw no need either to mince his words or to hedge his bets.

'All it doesn't say', said Crosby, 'is what was in that stuff he gave them.'

'Perhaps we shall find out,' said Sloan none too hopefully.

Both chemists were waiting for the policemen in the front entrance hall.

'I thought we'd adjourn to the conference room,' said George Gledhill as they clattered over the imitation classical black and white marble floor tiles. 'No one else is using it today.'

He led the way along a downstairs corridor and into a vast room built in the Anglo-French Renaissance style. There were Doric columns in scagliola at the far end and on one of the side walls a mahogany and brass scoring board.

'Used to be the billiard room,' explained Gledhill. 'Designed to keep the young gentlemen of the house away from the maids.'

'And the maidens,' contributed Itchen.

'Quite so,' said Detective Inspector Sloan austerely. 'Now, we have here a note of Dr Meggie's records and would like to know if the two patients who died yesterday and who were on the Cardigan Protocol had been having the test substance or the placebo.'

George Gledhill projected eagerness to help but it was Mike Itchen who unfolded the computer printout. 'If you can tell me the numbers on Paul Meggie's list – it's his first series, you understand.'

Crosby ran his finger down the paper. 'Galloway, Muriel, 4203.'

Itchen said 'Placebo', and Detective Inspector Sloan wondered then why it was that the police had an anonymous telephone call about her being on the drug programme and someone saw fit to write anti-research slogans on her son's garage door.

'And Granger, Abel, 3940,' read out Crosby.

'Ah,' said Mike Itchen. 'Granger was on the real McCoy.'

'They both died,' observed Sloan drily.

'They were both going to die anyway,' countered Gledhill swiftly.

'They had nothing to lose, you see,' Itchen came in antiphonally.

'Paul Meggie always hand-picked his candidates for any research he did. That was what made him the best man for this job,' said the Chief Chemist.

'Conscientious and discriminating,' supplemented Itchen like a Greek chorus.

'So Cardigan didn't do Abel Granger any good, then,' said Sloan. He was beginning to think it hadn't done Dr Meggie any good either but that was something different. 'And so,' he added, rather like the converse of a theorem, 'perhaps not having it did Muriel Galloway no harm, would you say?'

'Does – did – Dr Meggie put anything about that in his notes?' asked Gledhill circumspectly.

Sloan peered over Crosby's shoulder. 'Only that they both suffered an immediate and appreciable weight loss. Nothing more.'

Gledhill nodded sagely. 'That would help in heart failure, of course. Always does.'

'Less work for the heart to do,' chimed in Itchen, almost on cue.

'You understand, Inspector, that we should have liked a little more positive feedback from Dr Meggie than that.' The Chief Chemist leaned back in his chair. 'Here at Gilroy's we're at the leading edge of medical research.'

'I appreciate that,' said Sloan, unmoved. As far as he was concerned he was at the cutting edge of a search for a murderer and in his view edges didn't come more cutting than that.

'Now, we'd be all right,' lamented Gledhill, 'if we concentrated only on late-stage medicines.'

'Drugs for the dying, you mean?' asked Crosby suddenly coming to life.

'No, no.' Gledhill smiled thinly. 'Late-stage medicines are where nearly all of the groundwork has already been done and the efficacy proven.'

'Sometimes,' volunteered Itchen, 'they call them "me too" drugs.'

'Riding on someone else's research when the patent's expired,' explained Gledhill, 'or taking out a licence.'

'Not Gilroy's, though?' said Sloan, registering the fact that the firm wished to be considered as pure as driven snow.

'Not Gilroy's,' said Gledhill firmly.

'Here,' declared Itchen, 'we only do pure chemistry.'

'And original research,' chimed in George Gledhill. 'We don't go in for generic competition at all.'

'And', said Sloan gently, 'are you going to tell me the active ingredients of Cardigan now or are we going to have to get it analysed ourselves?'

'We'll tell you,' said Gledhill without hesitation. 'No problem there.'

'It's mainly an alkaloid from an Argentinian plant of the family *Rutaceae* called fagarine, which we're combining with one of the angiotension converting enzyme inhibitors,' reeled off Itchen.

If he was hoping to blind the two policemen with science he had failed. Crosby looked bored and Sloan had had that manoeuvre tried on him before by even cleverer people than these two.

'We're hoping that it will aid atrial fibrillation,' added Gledhill, 'but it's early days still—'

Sloan's mother, a great churchwoman in her day, always insisted that to the pure all things were pure. Sloan wasn't at all sure that Gilroy's Pharmaceuticals – pure scientists that they might be – came into that category. It wasn't that reservation, though, that stopped him leaving Gledhill and Itchen the copy of Dr Meggie's trials results when they asked him to.

It was the smell of fear caught by his fine-tuned detective nostrils.

*

It wasn't Saturday that was different for Mrs Hannah Glawari. It was morning. Her toilette was a lengthy affair and it was apparent that the arrival of two policemen had interrupted it. She had a vaguely dishevelled air about her as she showed them into the parlour.

She essayed an apologetic smile. 'I'm afraid it's a little early for me, officer.'

'We're sorry to trouble you, madam, but there are one or two points we'd like to clear up.'

While Mrs Glawari was clearly not naïve enough to believe this, she entered into the spirit of polite enquiry. 'Of course,' she murmured. 'Do sit down.'

'As you know,' began Sloan, 'we're looking into the death of Dr Paul Meggie.' He didn't know why 'looking into' seemed so much more anodyne than 'investigating' but it did.

'I'm glad to hear it,' said Mrs Glawari with a certain emphasis not lost on Detective Inspector Sloan. 'What is it exactly that you want to know?'

'Whether you have a car—'

'A little runabout, Inspector.'

'And whether you know the spot where Dr Meggie was found.'

She shook her head. 'I know', she said with a certain dignity, 'that people often go to a place with happy associations when they wish to end their lives, but the more I think about it the less like Paul that seems anyway—'

'And what we should also like', Sloan said, 'is a tape-recording of your voice.'

'My ordinary speaking voice?' she asked a little uncertainly.

'Just that, madam. Crosby, the tape machine, please.'

Dilys Chomel spent her Saturday morning in an agony of indecision. Dr Byville's patient without her spleen was now going downhill rather rapidly and it was frightening to see. The house physician's dilemma was whether or not to telephone Dr Byville and tell him so.

This would undoubtedly call down his wrath and result in scorn being heaped about her head. Unfortunately, Dr Byville was available and on call this weekend which meant she couldn't very well ring the more approachable Dr Beaumont instead – which was a pity. That would be a breach of medical etiquette – far more dangerous to her leaving testimonial than the deaths of any number of ill patients.

Sister Pocock wasn't a lot of help either. She belonged to the old school which regarded all young doctors as ignorant and foolish. As far as she was concerned, if Dr Byville had said the patient was going to die, then die the patient would. She even preached to her nurses that there was no disgrace in finding a patient dead 'as long as you don't find them cold'.

There would be no point in looking for help or comfort from that quarter.

No, what she would do was ring Dr Friar over at Kinnisport and share her fears with him. He would understand. He'd got a dying man on his ward too. A young one, to make it worse.

'See one, do one, teach one,' she murmured sadly to herself as she went to ring him.

But the switchboard at St Ninian's Hospital couldn't locate Dr Martin Friar and by the time a disconsolate Dr Dilys Chomel had got back to the Women's Medical Ward the patient without her spleen had died.

Detective Constable Crosby was not making a lot of headway either. He had been dispatched by Sloan to interview Darren Clements and his fellow animal rights campaigners. He had tracked the group down to a dim café near the railway station in Berebury. They were sitting in a huddle at the back, all very young and earnest.

'Why, if it isn't Mr Plod the Policeman!' called out Clements, his bandaged hand well to the fore.

'That's enough of that,' said Crosby.

'No law yet against being in a café, is there?' asked a thickset youth wearing glasses and with an open notebook before him on the table. The clever-sticks of the group, decided Crosby.

'No,' said Crosby. 'There's an old one against con-spiring to break the law though, or weren't you thinking of doing that?'

'What about the people who murder animals then?' shrilled a girl in black tights topped by some-thing resembling a frou-frou. 'Aren't they breaking the law, then?'

'Causing unnecessary suffering is against the law,' began Crosby, 'to animals, that is.' As far as he was concerned the same law should apply to humans, too – well, to policemen, anyway – but even in his short life he'd seen that it didn't.

'Tell that to the fox,' hissed another girl, 'before they blood someone with his blood.'

'And to the lambs going to the slaughter in those terrible lorries,' shuddered the first girl, her frou-frou quivering with indignation.

'What about the monkeys at Gilroy's?' demanded Darren Clements. 'How would you like to be cooped up behind bars like they are?'

With heroic restraint Detective Constable Crosby refrained from saying exactly who he would like to see behind bars. The boy with glasses and the note-book had the look of a barrack-room lawyer as well as leader about him and he didn't like to risk it.

'Perhaps,' sneered Cleversticks, 'you think people can do whatever they like as long as they don't frighten the horses. That's a quotation, in case you didn't know.'

Those were almost the exact sentiments, too, had Cleversticks known it, of the Mounted Police Division. Horses did not go fast enough for Crosby and he let it pass.

'Don't forget the factory-farmed pigs,' contributed another of Clements's cronies. He was wearing a gold ear-ring himself but no doubt would have objected to a pig being tagged.

'Pigs is equal,' announced the boy with glasses. 'That's a quotation, too,' he added hurriedly, not liking the expression on Crosby's face. 'George Orwell said it. Not me.'

'That's as maybe,' said Crosby grandly. 'What I want to know is whether Christopher Granger from Larking is one of your mob.'

'Why?'

'Never mind for why,' said Crosby magisterially. 'Was he or wasn't he?'

'We don't need to tell you,' snapped the bespectacled youth.

'Obstructing the police in the execution of their duty is an offence,' remarked Crosby.

'He was for a bit,' admitted Clements.

'Then he chickened out,' said she of the frou-frou contemptuously. 'No bottle.'

'Is he still one of you?' asked Crosby, getting out his own notebook.

'He stopped coming when the going got rough,' said one of the other girls. She, decided the constable, could be categorized as a born follower. Where Spectacles led, she would follow.

'Like when you started to break into Gilroy's?' suggested Crosby.

'Like whenever he wanted to,' she said carelessly, tossing her hair out of her eyes. 'It's a free world, isn't it?'

'Except for the animals!'

'Did you know', said Crosby, dredging up from his memory something he'd learned at the police training college, 'that they used to try animals when they'd killed some one or even stolen something?'

'I don't believe it,' said Clements indignantly. 'You're having us on.'

The boy with the glasses nodded with some reluctance. 'He's right. They had proper trials with judge and jury. Can't believe it, can you?'

'Barbarians,' said one of the young women.

'Disgusting,' said the other.

'What did they do when they found them guilty?' asked the born follower.

'Hanged them,' said Crosby, adding shamelessly as he got up to go, 'and then they ate them.'

Shirley Partridge had had her mid-morning coffee and had even managed a little chat with the artist in the front hall of St Ninian's Hospital. Funnily enough, Adrian Gomm's tattered jeans and deplorable old jumper did not worry her. And, anyway, as she meant to report to her mother later, he was ever so nice when she admired his painting.

She was just telling him that the colours at the bottom of the painting were ever so nice, although she didn't really like mice, when the Mayday call went out.

Shirley shot back to the switchboard as other people started to run overhead.

'Mayday! Lorkyn Ward!' Shirley put all the usual emergency procedures into operation. 'Cardiac arrest.' Automatically she put out calls for Dr Byville and Dr Beaumont in case either of them were still in the hospital. And sounded off the Senior Registrar's bleeper since Dr Martin Friar should definitely be in the hospital and on duty.

And when he didn't answer, she repeated the calls to his bleeper.

And when he still didn't answer, sounded them again and again.

Minutes later she had an anguished call from Lorkyn Ward. 'Switchboard, for God's sake can't you stop Dr Friar's bleeper – it's driving us mad.'

'Of course,' she said frostily. 'If you want me to—'

'He's the one with the cardiac arrest,' gasped a nurse. 'We think he's dead.'

Chapter Fifteen

Most people ... fall back on the old rule that if you cannot have what you believe in you must believe in what you have.

'Dead?' howled Superintendent Leeyes, quite affronted. 'He can't be.'

'Cardiac arrest,' said Detective Inspector Sloan succinctly. He had not shared Dr Dilys Chomel's inhibitions about disturbing the great and the good when they were off-duty and had promptly apprised his senior officer of the news about Dr Martin Friar, Saturday morning or not. It had not made for popularity.

'And are you anywhere nearer the other sort of arrest?' demanded Leeyes trenchantly.

'We've cleared away some of the undergrowth,' said Sloan obliquely, lapsing into horticultural vernacular. 'I think the Merry Widow's in the clear because she would have been better off if Paul Meggie had lived to sign that Will in Expectation of marriage that Puckle, Puckle and Nunnery were drawing up for him—'

'Always presuming that she didn't know it hadn't been signed.' The superintendent could always find an objection.

'And the daughter,' persisted Sloan, 'I would assume, would have been the one to have been disadvantaged by its being signed.' He added his own caveat before the superintendent did. 'Always presuming she knew anything about it at all.'

Leeyes snorted. 'I don't know what's going on, Sloan, but I don't like it.'

'It may be natural causes,' said Sloan, who did not understand what had been going on either and was sure he wouldn't like it when he did, 'although nothing has been said about Martin Friar having been ill before.'

'And we still don't know if the Cardigan Protocol had anything to do with yesterday's two deaths.'

'Not Muriel Galloway's anyway,' said Sloan, 'because according to Gilroy's records she wasn't on the stuff in the first place. As to Abel Granger—'

'Yes?'

'Dr Dabbe took some specimens for analysis so we don't know yet.'

'Where's our friendly neighbourhood pathologist now, might I ask?'

Sloan shot a look at his watch. 'About level with Cranberry Point, I should say.'

'Where!'

'I should imagine that by this time, sir, he'll be making for the Cunliffe Gap.'

'You mean,' he said with rising indignation, 'he's out in a boat?'

'Well out,' said Sloan. 'And heading for the open sea.' And if he knew Dr Hector Smithson Dabbe, ahead of the field too; if 'field' was what you called the entrants of a yachting race.

'Hasn't he got a ship-to-shore radio telephone?' That was old technology, not new. The superintendent was opposed to all new technology on principle.

'We've tried that, sir.' Sloan coughed. 'I understand that Dr Dabbe didn't take any form of communication with him.' The pathologist was nobody's fool.

'We'll get the helicopter to pick him off his yacht then,' vowed the superintendent. 'Time it earned its oats. That'd get it away from Traffic Division for a change and a good thing, too.'

'I very much doubt if Dr Dabbe would consider jumping ship—'

'Well,' growled Leeyes, 'whatever you do, don't you let that moron of a deputy of his lay a finger on that body until Dabbe comes back.'

'No, sir,' said Sloan, although he wasn't at all sure how he was going to accomplish this.

'It's not death from natural causes,' snarled

Leeyes, 'until Dabbe says so. Is that clearly understood?'

'Yes, sir. I am told,' advanced Sloan cautiously, 'by the Administrator at the hospital at Kinnisport where Dr Friar worked, that sudden death from heart attack is not uncommon these days in overworked and highly stressed junior doctors.'

Superintendent Leeyes, whose view of administrators was not high, grunted.

'He was also', carried on Sloan, 'being expected to – er – hold the fort as a consequence of Dr Meggie's sudden death as well as do his usual work for Dr Byville and some for Dr Beaumont.'

'Did he just keel over or something?' enquired Leeyes in a detached way. He took the view that other people's workloads – whatever they were – were always lighter than his own.

'He called his boss, Dr Byville, out to see a dying patient this morning and did a very short ward round with him and he was taken ill some time later.'

'Too many people altogether dying for my liking,' remarked Leeyes.

'And,' continued Sloan doggedly, 'as far as we can ascertain at this stage—'

'Sloan—' began Leeyes dangerously.

'Find out,' amended Sloan on the instant, 'some of them were going to die anyway.'

Superintendent Leeyes said that he didn't see what that had got to do with it, and delivered his own apotheosis on the point. 'What matters is whether they died when they shouldn't have done. Of if they died because someone else wanted them to. That's the law, Sloan. You should know that.'

'Yes, indeed, sir.' He didn't doubt that this would be the legal view. It was the more pragmatic medical one that worried him. He was not at all sure now that it would be the same as the legal one. 'The problem is that Dr Meggie's death is the only one so far that we have what you might call valid reservations about.'

He was talking to the wrong man.

'Valid reservations, Sloan?' exploded Leeyes. 'People are dying like flies all around us and you go on about valid reservations! The place is like a shambles except that there isn't any blood. You'd better get busy.'

Saturdays were less different on the farm than they were at either the hospital or the police station. It was the seasons that changed the pattern of work there rather than any arbitrary divisions made by man. Christopher and Simon Granger each had their own duties at Willow End Farm and duly went about them during the morning while their mother and married sister gradually turned their thoughts from a dying man and towards a country funeral.

Unspoken but hanging about the second generation was a miasma of uncertainty about their father's will. Since they would have all thought it unseemly to discuss this before he was decently interred with his forefathers in Larking churchyard they spent their time in a leaderless hiatus; each thinking their own private thoughts.

Old Mrs Granger thought chiefly – and without affection – about Simon's wife because it was to her that she knew she would presently be surrendering her home. She knew enough though now about the role of a farmer's wife to know that it was too demanding a one for a farmer's mother and had her eye on a small bungalow with central heating near Larking Church. There would be room there for Christopher if he wanted to come with her.

Simon Granger had had enough sense to keep his wife out of the way for the time being. Time enough for her to come into her own when his mother had made her intentions clear. In between inspecting the hay he mulled over what his father's testamentary dispositions might be. Come what may, he reckoned his sister would come out best. She'd be able to get her portion and go back home to her husband and children without a care.

Christopher Granger walked over to inspect the bullocks, wondering if Simon would want to buy him out and toying with the idea of what he would do if he did. He knew now with a new unexpected certainty that he himself would never want to buy

Simon out and saddle himself with debt for as far
ahead as he could see.

He'd rather sell up than that.

With some capital he could live for a year or two
while he did the one thing he'd always really wanted
to do – go to art college and paint.

Idly he wondered if Simon would instead suggest
paying him his share of the farm's income. That
would be something to consider. Better for Simon
than going to the bank – if Dad had left it that way,
of course. And then there was his mother and sister
to think about. A hard man his father had been but
a fair one. Perhaps he needn't worry after all. Dad
would have done what was best for family and farm,
he could be sure.

Today he decided to approach the bullocks from
above. He walked along the hill above the valley of
the stream. He edged his way round the top field
and found himself looking down on to the little
patch of grass by the willows where yesterday
there had been that car. It wasn't there now because
yesterday evening the police had covered it in
tarpaulins and notices about not touching anything
and very carefully put it on a low-loader and taken
it away.

Now there was nothing but a little flattened grass
and tyre marks to show where it had been and where
a man had died. A glint of movement over to his
left caught his eye and he saw a tiny car – it looked

like a child's toy at this distance – snaking its way up the farm road.

At this distance he could see that it was the maroon-coloured vehicle the rector drove and that it was heading for the farm house. Christopher Granger stood there irresolutely for a little while and then turned on his heel and started back towards home.

There was something he had to tell the police.

Even Dr Byville's legendary medical composure appeared to have been shaken by the sudden death of his registrar.

'I was only talking to the fellow a couple of hours ago,' he said to Sloan and Crosby when he had been retrieved from a consulting session at the private clinic to join the two policemen at Kinnisport Hospital. 'Doesn't seem possible.'

'He was all right then, I take it?' murmured Sloan. They were all three in the sister's office of Lorkyn Ward which was where Dr Martin Friar had expired.

The Consultant Physician paused before he answered. 'Yes and no, Inspector. He did say something to me about thinking he might've got an infection on the way though he couldn't very well have gone off duty in the circumstances.'

'Ah—'

'He said his chest was feeling a bit tight and so forth but that he was quite well enough to keep going.' Byville grimaced. 'What he told me was that he'd take an aspirin or something as he didn't want to start on a course of antibiotics if it wasn't anything—'

'Only it was something,' intoned Crosby, 'wasn't it?'

'God, yes! He must have been cooking a coronary thrombosis all along.' Byville started to doodle on a pad on sister's desk. 'I must confess I didn't think anything of it at the time but now—'

Now, Sloan would have been the first to concede, was different from then. It almost always was.

'Not surprising, of course,' went on Byville, 'that he should have a coronary. Paul Meggie's death had undoubtedly started to get to him—'

'As well it might,' contributed Sloan.

'And I must say the death in the ward this morning wasn't a nice one.'

'Was that patient on the Cardigan Protocol, too?' asked Crosby.

Byville shook his head. 'No, it was a spleen, not a heart case. Different ball game altogether and miles away, you understand, from the cardiac system anatomically speaking.'

'I see, sir,' said Sloan. It was not strictly true that he saw. The human anatomy that policemen were taught – and learned later – was of a very basic variety. In more ways than one.

'We'll have to wait for the *post mortem* to be sure, of course,' carried on Byville worriedly. 'He might have had an aortic aneurysm, for instance, or another of that sort of time-bomb type of condition which is just waiting to happen without anyone knowing that it's there.' He frowned. 'They're beginning to talk in the literature of something called Adult Sudden Death Syndrome now.' His shoulders sagged. 'It's no use our second guessing, Inspector, or theorizing ahead of the facts either.'

'No, Doctor,' agreed Detective Inspector Sloan. This was part of his own credo, too, if not his superintendent's.

Just then the door opened and the ward sister came in. 'Yes, Sister,' Sloan said. 'What is it? I'm sorry we had to commandeer your office—'

This nurse was no Florentinian battle-axe left over from the Crimea. She was youngish and patently more than a little frightened. She came and stood uncertainly in the middle of the room. Sloan didn't know to which of them she intended to speak and in fact she avoided all their eyes by addressing the floor.

'It's the Cardigan Protocol bottles—'

'What about them?' demanded Dr Byville sharply.

'Three of them are missing from the ward drug

cabinet,' she said, flustered and a little breathless. 'I've just checked.'

'The bloody fool,' said Byville compassionately. 'The poor bloody fool.'

Chapter Sixteen

All that can be said for medical popularity is that until there is a practicable alternative to blind trust in the doctor the truth about the doctor is so terrible that we dare not face it.

'Where to now sir?' asked Detective Constable Crosby as the two policemen clattered down the stone staircase of the old local authority hospital at Kinnisport.

'The car,' said Sloan tersely. 'I need to sit and think. Come along.'

'Yes, sir,' said Crosby, pausing out of sheer habit to look at the mural on his way across the entrance hall. He regarded what was being painted and called up dubiously, 'That a vase?'

'It's what's called an alembic, mate.' Adrian Gomm looked down on them both from his ladder. 'It's the sort of vessel in which they used to try to sell the secret of eternal life in Chaucer's day.'

'Haven't found it yet, have they?' riposted Crosby. 'Not in this place, anyway.'

'A little thing like that didn't stop 'em trying to sell it,' said the artist cheerfully. 'You should know that. People were gullible then and they're gullible now.'

'That's something different—' Crosby showed a tendency to argue as Sloan urged him on his way.

'If that's your car by the front door,' said Adrian Gomm, peering through an upper window, 'then there's some kids out there looking as if they'd like to try it on for size.'

As a manoeuvre, that worked quicker and Sloan was soon sitting in the relative privacy of the police car. Superintendent Leeyes would have to be kept in the picture, of course, but not before he had first tried to work one or two things out for himself.

Sloan had settled his frame in the front passenger seat, and stretched his legs out as far as they would go. 'There's something, somewhere, that we're not getting, Crosby. Things do not add up whichever way they are looked at.' He hesitated, thinking aloud. 'There's almost too much that doesn't fit.'

'A crystal ball would come in handy,' volunteered Crosby unhelpfully.

'And one of the things I can't understand', mused Sloan, 'is where the woman in the case comes in.'

'*Cherchez la femme,*' said Crosby, still unhelpful.

'All the telephone calls we can't trace were made by a woman, remember?'

'For my money,' said Crosby largely, 'Bunty Meggie is the one with means, motive and opportunity.'

'Why should she get steamed up about animal rights and put something on the Galloways' garage doors?'

'A blind,' pronounced Crosby.

'I think', said Sloan, 'that it would be useful to have a tape-recording of the voices of all of them, including Shirley Partridge. She sent for us quickly enough when Dr Friar collapsed. We mightn't have been told for ages . . . oh, and those girls with Darren Clements and his crowd—'

'They don't talk,' said Crosby feelingly. 'They shriek.'

'And Dr Dilys Chomel,' said Sloan. 'The girl on the switchboard said she'd been in touch with Martin Friar more than once today because she'd made the telephone connection—'

Crosby hitched a shoulder up under his seat-belt. 'No. I talked to Dr Chomel about that and she said they only discussed the spleen patient who died on Lorkyn Ward this morning. Apparently she knew the man because he'd started off in Berebury Hospital and then got transferred over to St Ninian's not long before he died.'

'She was looking after some of Dr Meggie's

Cardigan Protocol patients as well though, don't forget.'

'Perhaps that's a blind, too,' said Crosby. 'The medics go in for double-blind trials, don't they?'

'As for the Merry Widow—'

'She could have been luring him to his doom,' said Crosby. 'Him and anyone else.'

'Siren voices, all of them,' remarked Sloan absently.

'Pardon, sir?'

'The sirens', Sloan informed him, his mind on something else, 'were sea nymphs whose songs were irresistible to men. They lured sailors on to the rocks.'

'Christopher Granger's a bit of a wet,' said Crosby, whose line of thought was not too difficult to follow, 'but his voice is all right.'

'Dr Byville thought with Dr Friar it might have been a case of his doing a bit of experimental work on the Cardigan Protocol all on his own.'

Detective Constable Crosby had inserted himself into the driver's seat and now started to play about with the radio. 'Making his own name by finding out for himself what was wrong with Cardigan? That was what Dr Byville meant, wasn't it, sir?'

'It's been done before,' said Sloan, his mind going back to the library at his old school. There had been a painting there of Dr Edward Jenner vaccinating his own son against smallpox. What had struck Sloan then was that there had been no sign anywhere in the picture of an anguished and protesting Mrs Edward Jenner looking on. His own mother would never have let any doctor try out something new on him for the sake of experiment and he supposed most mothers would feel the same. Perhaps Dr Jenner hadn't told Mrs Jenner what he proposed to do to their son. That would have been one way round the difficulty. Now they had something called 'informed consent', didn't they?

'Some people will do anything to hit the headlines,' said Crosby censoriously.

'Fame is the spur,' agreed Sloan.

If the picture was still there the present generation of schoolboys probably thought it was a depiction of a youth being initiated by a drug-pusher.

'Not worth it,' said Crosby confidently. 'You're a long time dead.'

The radio in the police car crackled and suddenly came to life. The disembodied, slightly nasal voice of the operator at Berebury interrupted them. 'A message has been received from a Christopher Granger of Willow End Farm, Larking—'

'Receiving you,' said Crosby, sitting up, his hand on the ignition switch.

'He says,' said the voice, 'that he wishes to talk to Detective Inspector Sloan about the late Dr Paul Meggie.'

'He does, does he?' muttered Sloan out of earshot

of the microphone. 'Well, in that case we'd like to talk to him.'

In fact talking to Christopher Granger was made easier by the young farmer's eagerness to say what he had to say. The words tumbled out.

'I wonder if you'd mind repeating that, sir?' said Detective Inspector Sloan in tones of arctic formality.

'I'm sorry,' said Christopher Granger readily. 'I thought you'd understood.'

'I think I did,' said Sloan grimly.

'When I found Dr Meggie's car,' said Christopher Granger all over again, 'not of course that I knew it was Dr Meggie's car at the time, you understand—'

'I understand,' ground Sloan between clenched teeth. 'Go on.'

'There was something lying on top of that folder on the passenger seat that you took away.'

'That's what I thought you said.'

'It was a piece of stiff paper – almost cardboard – with this slogan written on it.'

'Which said?' Sloan's pen was in his hand.

Christopher Granger had the grace to look embarrassed. ' "No tests on dumb animals".' He hesitated. 'It was written in red like it was blood, with drips drawn down from the letters.'

At this moment the only blood Sloan wanted

was Christopher Granger's but a long, long training prevented him from saying so.

'I know I shouldn't have touched it, Inspector, but I didn't think at the time—'

'That's true,' said Sloan peremptorily. 'You didn't. But you've thought now, have you?'

'All I knew', he flushed miserably, 'was that I'd come in for enough flak as it was from everyone on the farm for how I felt about cruelty to livestock and I didn't think I could take any more, not with Dad dying and everything—'

'Proper little mother's helper, isn't he, sir?' said Crosby as they left a considerably chastened Christopher Granger at the farmhouse and started back down to the main road.

'He might at least have kept that paper and given Forensics a chance,' returned Sloan, 'instead of just dropping it in the stream.'

Crosby jerked his head. 'Not that we'd be a lot further forward if we did have it in our hands that I can see.'

'We could've compared the writing with the graffiti on Gordon Galloway's garage door,' said Sloan, since he was, after all supposed to be teaching the constable something. On his part Crosby was supposed to be learning something – but that was different. 'It would be evidence,' he went on bitterly. 'Do you realize, Crosby, that the only hard evidence we've got in this case so far are some tiny blisters round Dr Meggie's mouth—'

'And another doctor's body,' broke in the constable.

'Cause of death so far unknown,' said Sloan flatly. 'And likely to remain so until Dr Dabbe gets back to dry land.'

'There's the Cardigan Protocol,' said Crosby, slowing up for the junction with the metalled road. 'Where to, sir?'

'Headquarters,' said Sloan without enthusiasm. Superintendent Leeyes would have to be disturbed on a Saturday all over again. And it was odds on that he wouldn't like it. That quotation about the pitcher going to the well once too often had more than a ring of truth to it as far as the superintendent was concerned. 'And as for the Cardigan Protocol, Crosby, Mrs Galloway didn't have the real stuff and died, and Abel Granger did have it and also died. Martin Friar may or not have had it and may or may not have died from an overdose of it if he did.'

'That must prove something, sir,' said Crosby, touching the accelerator.

'I dare say it does,' said Sloan acidly, 'but you tell me what.'

Crosby paused for thought. 'That whoever wrote those words on Gordon Galloway's door and rung us up to say she was on a drug trial didn't know she wasn't on the real thing or wanted us to think she was?'

'That's a possibility,' admitted Sloan fairly. 'Or if one person wrote the slogan and a different person rung, not one and the same, then neither of them did.'

Crosby tried again. 'That the Cardigan Protocol didn't make a blind bit of difference?'

'That's another possibility, although something made a big difference to Dr Martin Friar,' observed Sloan bleakly as the police car picked up speed. 'But what?'

'Three doses of Cardigan?' suggested Crosby, spotting a milk tanker ahead and moving out to position the car for overtaking on the narrow country road.

'Since we have got no further with our investigations,' began Sloan acidly, 'I am in no particular hurry to get back to Berebury, let alone to meet my Maker.'

'No, sir,' agreed Crosby, abating the car's speed not at all and getting ready to perform a virtuoso manoeuvre round the other vehicle. 'Don't worry, sir.'

'There is therefore no need for party tricks at the wheel,' said Sloan urgently.

'Sorry, sir.'

Sloan wasn't listening. He was suddenly thinking about party tricks. Last Christmas he'd been the one to collect his infant son from a children's party while his wife, Margaret, did some Christmas shopping of her own. He'd got there early. And he'd been in time to see the bluff, gruff Father Christmas turn his back on the children for a moment, then face them again. Throwing off his red robe and pulling off his white beard and revealing a white satin outfit underneath, he had turned himself into the fairy at the top of the Christmas tree. It had only been when he spoke again – this time in a high feminine voice – that the little children had been convinced of what a wand could do.

It hadn't been a wand that had turned a man's voice into a woman's one: and this particular father had taken the trouble to find out what had completed the party trick.

A few breaths of the gas helium.

When Detective Inspector Sloan next looked up, the milk tanker was nowhere to be seen and the lure of the open road was exerting its usual effect on Crosby's speed.

'I've changed my mind', said Sloan, 'about going back to Berebury. Head for Staple St James—'

He very nearly added something about not sparing the horses, James, but with Crosby at the wheel decided against it. He wanted to live to catch a murderer.

Chapter Seventeen

The man who does evil skilfully, energetically, master-fully, grows prouder and bolder at every crime.

Detective Inspector Sloan looked up at the sky as an alternative to looking at the road ahead while Crosby was at the wheel. The only thing that the detective constable really enjoyed was driving fast cars fast, which was precisely why Inspector Harpe would not have him in Traffic Division.

Sloan noted that the sky was clear except for a few high clouds but there was a good stiff breeze bending the treetops, which was just exactly what Dr Dabbe would have wanted for his sailing race. Fair stood the wind for the pathologist, all right, but all the same Sloan would be glad when the doctor was safely back on the job at his mortuary table. It wasn't that he would be unbearably surprised to learn that young Dr Friar had died from an overdose of whatever was in the Cardigan Protocol. He knew only too well that too much of anything – including alcohol – meant to cure could be fatal. Equally, he wouldn't be bowled over to learn instead that the doctor had had a heart attack – but the police did need to know which – and soon.

Sloan took another look at the sky. He wasn't quite so sure how favourable the conditions were for two policemen on their way to a pharmaceutical research firm but time would tell if they were propitious for detection.

As the police car turned off the main road towards the village of Staple St James something Dr Dabbe had said came into Sloan's mind. The pathologist had thought that, showman or not, Dr Meggie had been a good doctor. It was a tiny little fact in a case that was, so far, noticeably short on hard fact. Although its significance – if it was significant – had so far escaped him, Detective Inspector Sloan conscientiously took it into consideration.

'Sorry, Crosby, I didn't quite catch that.' Actually, he hadn't even realized the constable had been speaking. They had arrived at Gilroy's place at Staple St James without his noticing.

'Which way in, sir? Back door or front?'

'Back.' This was no time for niceties.

In the nature of things policemen become specialists in measuring degrees of fear. When Detective Inspector Sloan had interviewed George Gledhill and Mike Itchen earlier that morning he had known that he had been talking to two frightened men. Now they were aware of Dr Friar's death and he, Sloan, knew that he was talking to two very frightened men indeed.

Fear, of course, was an emotion that took people differently. There were those who became practically catatonic, paralysed to the point of being unresponsive to the most skilled police interrogation. Others couldn't stop talking, their tongues loosened by an anxiety too great to handle.

As it happened Gledhill was inclined to silence and Itchen to speech. Sloan took a policy decision about interviewing them separately. If he talked to one man alone, the other would have time to think. He didn't want that to happen.

Uninvited he pulled up a chair in Gledhill's office and said cosily that it was time for a chat. 'A real chat,' he added.

'About what?' managed Itchen, licking lips that were obviously dry.

'Let's start with the Cardigan Protocol, shall we?'

'Nothing to add to what we told you earlier.' Gledhill was quite taciturn.

'What would be the fatal dose, would you say?' asked Sloan, eyeing them both. 'We shall of course be doing a full analysis ourselves—'

The two scientists exchanged glances. It was the Chief Chemist who spoke. 'That would depend in the first place on the condition of the patient,' said Gledhill.

'Shall we postulate a perfectly healthy young male?' said Sloan. From where he was sitting he could see over Gledhill's shoulder into the garden. The maze was prominent in the foreground.

'If any substance had been taken on an empty stomach,' said Itchen, 'it would have made a difference—'

'So?' persisted Sloan. This case, he decided, had a lot in common with a maze. Each and every new pathway except one led up a blind alley. The trick was to find the right pathway at every turn.

Itchen spoke with obvious reluctance. 'Half-a-dozen tablets, say, would probably be enough to set up a fatal hypotension.'

'And the number of tablets in each bottle of the Cardigan Protocol?' asked Sloan.

'Ten,' said Gledhill, his expression strained.

'That's the real tablets, not the placebo,' put in Itchen, who was looking distinctly white about the gills.

'Like Russian roulette, isn't it?' observed Crosby chattily.

Nobody smiled.

'Are you – er – postulating that that is what killed Dr Friar, Inspector?' asked Itchen.

'I'm asking questions about a number of anomalies,' returned Sloan crisply. 'Tell me, who else on the staff of St Ninian's and Berebury Hospitals has been doing work for you?'

There was something almost palpable about the way in which both men relaxed at the change of tack. Gledhill's tenseness eased and Itchen, his colour returning, started to resume some of his laid-back style. This, Sloan noted, was obviously safe ground for them. He would go back to the dangerous places in a moment and catch them off-guard.

'Dr Hulbert checked some data for us. Haematology's his speciality,' offered Itchen, 'but then—'

'Then he married money and lost interest in the extra work,' finished Gledhill.

'And Dr Beaumont's never cared for research. Says he's busy enough getting the work done properly and—' Itchen was still the more voluble of the two men.

This was something Detective Inspector Sloan understood. Down at the police station they had those who saw everything as a statistic and those who got on with the job. 'And?'

'And there's Dr Byville, of course,' said Itchen, 'but he's not doing anything for Gilroy's at the moment.'

Gledhill said, 'Dr Byville put up a research project to the Committee but they turned it down last month.'

'Oh?'

'A comparison trial on post-splenectomy patients,' said Gledhill readily enough.

'We've got a promising drug,' chimed in Itchen,

'for preventing placenta praevia but Mr Maldonson's making too much money as it is to want to do a controlled trial.'

'What will you do about that?' Sloan was always interested in how other people solved their problems.

'We're getting a younger man in Luston to do it for us,' replied Itchen. Luston was in a decidedly more workaday part of Calleshire than Berebury.

George Gledhill leaned over and began rather tentatively, 'Inspector, should there be anything about Dr Meggie's or Dr Friar's deaths that you think we should know, would you—'

Detective Inspector Sloan wasn't listening. He was staring out at the maze, his mind elsewhere.

Suddenly he reached across Gledhill's desk and picked up his telephone. 'This an outside line?'

The Chief Chemist nodded.

Sloan dialled an emergency number. 'Get me Berebury Hospital,' he barked. 'I need to talk to Dr Dilys Chomel. And quickly.' He pointed at both scientists. 'You stay here. Crosby, you get the car started. We need to move quickly.'

'No, Tracy, of course Dr Chomel's not over here,' said Shirley Partridge on the Kinnisport switchboard. 'She never comes over here. You know that.'

The land-line crackled.

'I know it's urgent,' protested Shirley, 'but there's nothing I can do about it.'

'I've rung every single person I can think of,' said young Tracy over at Berebury Hospital, 'but nobody seems to know where she is. I've sounded her bleeper for her until I'm sick of it but the policeman sounded so upset when I couldn't get hold of her that I thought I'd better carry on.'

'A good idea,' said Shirley Partridge wisely. 'You never know, do you?'

'Neither of the medical wards can trace her,' Tracy sounded quite flurried, 'and Sister Pocock's off-duty this afternoon.'

'What about the staff nurse?' After all these years Shirley knew her lines of command.

'Hasn't seen her since the end of the morning. Seems Dr Chomel was very put out when she heard about poor Dr Friar.'

'I don't blame her,' said Shirley Partridge, who had not only been very put out herself, too, but hadn't yet been home to tell her mother about it.

'The others didn't know him so well, of course,' said Tracy, 'with him really being over with you at Kinnisport.'

'Whatever they said about him,' pronounced Shirley Partridge, generously overlooking the matter of Dr Friar's shirt sleeves, 'he was too young to die.'

*

'Can't you go any faster, Crosby?' Detective Inspector Sloan wasn't looking at the sky now. 'She's too young to die.'

Rightly taking this question as rhetorical, Detective Constable Crosby, racing driver *manqué*, took a corner in a manner that, had Inspector Harpe seen him, would have kept him out of Traffic Division for ever.

He pulled the police car out of the road from Staple St James on to the main road with a mere token glance in both directions and put his foot down before he said, 'Where to exactly, sir?'

'Berebury Hospital,' came back Sloan, 'to try to find someone who might know where to find Dr Dilys Chomel.'

Crouching over the wheel, a cross between Jehu and Mr Toad of Toad Hall, Crosby bent his mind to covering the distance, while Detective Inspector Sloan addressed himself over the car radio to every police officer in 'F' Division.

'Seek and detain a young African woman doctor by the name of Dilys Chomel. Five feet seven inches tall, well built with excellent carriage—' He changed his tone for an aside. 'What did you say her hair was like, Crosby?'

'Rats' tails with curls,' said that young man. 'Lots of them, all hanging down.'

'They may save her life,' said Sloan seriously.

'How come?' asked Crosby, effortlessly executing a *pas de deux* between two lorries.

'More easily recognized,' said Sloan tersely, turning back to speak into the microphone. 'Also needed urgently for interview is Sister Pocock of the Female Medical Ward of Berebury Hospital, present whereabouts also unknown.'

In the event Sister Pocock was located first and quite quickly. She was spotted from a patrol car stepping out of the hospital in mufti on her way home for the weekend.

'Get her to the microphone,' implored Sloan as Crosby performed a slalom manoeuvre round a traffic chicane. 'I need to talk to her quickly.'

Sister Pocock might have been an old battle-axe but she was also highly experienced in responding first and asking questions or – sometimes, more importantly – not asking questions afterwards.

'Dr Chomel was given a lift down to the town this afternoon,' she said in her precise, calm manner, 'by someone to whom she had expressed a wish to be shown an old-fashioned barber's pole. We happened to be talking about this one day in my office. I understand the caller knew of one in the High Street.'

'Where in the High Street?' demanded Sloan. Berebury High Street was long and, on a Saturday afternoon, seething with people.

But that Sister Pocock could not say. She herself

went to the hairdressing salon on the corner by the church, if that was any help.

'I know the one with the pole,' said Crosby, changing gear and turning the car round at speed. 'I don't go there myself, mind you, sir. It's one of those funny places where everyone goes.'

'Unisex,' divined Sloan. 'Then it's the one the other side of the river bridge.'

'He may not have taken her there,' began Crosby.

'Too dangerous not to,' said Sloan. 'He'll go there first and be seen with her there and then dump her afterwards. Don't hang about, man. We haven't got all day.'

Crosby gave the accelerator pedal a joyous push and shot up the High Street, the police car's two-tone horn blaring and its blue light flashing.

Afterwards Detective Inspector Sloan on mature reflection was among the first to admit that a quieter approach might have been better. As it was Dr Roger Byville heard the police car's siren, and turned his head in its direction. In one swift movement he pushed Dr Dilys Chomel out of his way and started to thread his way as speedily as he could through the shoppers in the crowded street.

Elbowing his way past first one and then another with scant ceremony, it was soon clear which way he was heading. The progress of the police car through the multitude was even more hampered by the pedestrians instantly turning into fascinated bystanders. Not only did they slow the vehicle down but their very numbers obstructed Sloan's view of the man.

He tumbled out of the car and started running towards the river after his quarry. 'Get the girl,' he shouted at Crosby, as Byville made a last sprint towards the promenade along the riverside. 'And stop him,' he roared to the crowd, as he tore after Byville.

The doctor turned and looked over his shoulder, putting on an even greater spurt as Sloan closed in on him. The detective inspector caught the flapping tail of Byville's jacket but before he could get a better grip of the man, he had eeled his way out of the garment, leaving Sloan grasping an empty sleeve.

The policeman lost a precious second there and Byville reached the iron railing with a clear lead on him. He vaulted over it into the river as Sloan hurtled fruitlessly after him over the paving stones of the promenade.

Even as Byville hit the water Sloan saw a youth on the bridge struggle out of his jacket and kick his shoes off. The young man steadied himself on the bridge parapet for a moment in the manner of a practised swimmer and dived in after the man in the river.

Chapter Eighteen

Juries seldom notice facts and they have been taught to regard any doubts of the omniscience and omnipotence of doctors as blasphemy.

'The problem, sir,' explained Detective Inspector Sloan expansively, 'was that almost everything we thought was important was quite irrelevant.'

'It would be very helpful, Sloan,' said Superintendent Leeyes, who could probably have taught Genghis Khan a thing or two about assertion techniques, 'if you would refrain from talking in riddles.'

It was the Monday morning and they were in the superintendent's office in Berebury Police Station.

'Yes, sir.' He waved his hand over a stack of notebooks and reports. 'Let me put it like this. Nothing that we had actually been investigating had anything whatsoever to do with the real cause of the matter.'

'Say that again, Sloan.'

'That goes for animal liberationists, Dr Meggie's – er – domestic problems and even the famous Cardigan Protocol. Mind you, sir, they were all deliberately made to seem very important by the murderer.'

Unfortunately this unequivocal statement did not make the superintendent any happier. 'And how then', asked Leeyes, in the last resort a self-preservationist, 'do I explain the waste of police time while you were playing about with them?'

'You could put it down to the workings of a highly trained mind,' suggested Sloan. 'That of Dr Roger Byville.'

How clever that mind had actually been Sloan had not really started to work out until after the doctor and his rescuer had been brought out of the river, both very wet. The doctor was taken into custody, his rescuer borne shoulder high to the Dog and Duck.

Sloan's first visit after that had been to Berebury Hospital. A shocked but still game Dr Dilys Chomel had done her best to answer his questions.

'Yes,' she said, puzzled but alert, 'we admitted here all of Dr Roger Byville's patients who had had their spleens removed for any reason.'

'But they didn't do very well?' suggested Sloan. He pulled himself up with a jerk. He shouldn't be talking like the doctors did. He rephrased the question in police plain-speak. 'Many of them died?'

She nodded, her long curls swinging. 'Yes and he told me they would. He said that he was very interested in the treatment of post-splenectomy cases but he should warn me that they were very prone to overwhelming infection and that we would lose more patients than we saved.'

Dilys Chomel could still not bring herself to use Roger Byville's name more than she had to.

'And as far as you know this will be borne out by the records on both the Male and Female Medical Wards here?' Even now there were trained medical-records staff working through these. Sloan had not failed to note the simple satisfaction it had given the nursing staff to call the Administrator in to work on a Saturday afternoon to ruin other weekends to arrange for this task to be done.

'Oh, yes, Inspector. Even the young man we shipped over to Kinnisport died.'

'That', said Detective Inspector Sloan soberly, 'was the whole trouble.' Early indications from those trained staff who were going through the records of the medical wards at Kinnisport Hospital suggested that the patients admitted there usually lived.

'I don't understand—.'

'But Dr Byville thought you might have done and that was why you were in such danger, Doctor.' If the girl hadn't been fully fledged as a medico yesterday, she certainly was today.

'I still don't understand—'

'And I think', said Sloan, pursuing his own line of thought, 'that we may assume that Dr Martin Friar – like Dr Meggie – had noticed what was going on.'

'But', she cried, 'I still don't know what that was.'

Detective Inspector Sloan did. Now.

'Dr Byville had been refused permission by the Ethics Committee to do some comparison trials – that's where you treat two comparable groups of patients with the same condition with two different drugs, isn't it?'

'Yes, yes,' she said, some of her own confidence beginning to return. 'Go on.'

'So,' said Sloan, 'I reckon that he gave his patients at Kinnisport Hospital one set of drugs—'

She sat up. 'They lived. Martin had noticed that. He told me.'

'And those patients here at Berebury Hospital were given another lot of drugs entirely.'

'And they died,' said the house physician sadly. 'I can tell you that.'

'And then,' said Detective Inspector Sloan, 'along comes this young man whom you had here who asked to be transferred over to Kinnisport to be nearer his family.'

She clapped her hands to her forehead. 'I remember Martin saying Dr Byville was cross about that.'

'I'll bet he was,' said Sloan warmly. 'That not only spoilt his series but put his scheme at risk of being discovered by Martin Friar.'

Dilys Chomel looked him squarely in the face. 'Are you telling me, Inspector, that Dr Meggie had already tumbled to it?'

He nodded. 'That's what we think. Dr Meggie, like most of the other consultants, had beds at both hospitals and his, being medical as well, were in the same wards.'

'Dr Meggie was a good doctor,' she said, unconsciously echoing Dr Dabbe. 'He wouldn't have sat back and done nothing if he had thought something was wrong—'

'No.'

'And neither', she said stoutly, 'would poor Martin.'

'Which', repeated Sloan later on to Superintendent Leeyes, 'is why they both had to die. At least,' added Sloan, 'I think to be strictly honest, sir, Dr Friar didn't have to die.' It was something that was worrying him.

'What's that, Sloan?' Leeyes's head came up with a jerk. 'What's that supposed to mean?'

'I should have spotted much sooner that only someone who knew the set-up and that Martin Friar was Dr Meggie's senior registrar would have rung the hospital at Kinnisport on Friday morning about changing the clinic.'

'Anyone could have found that out,' said Leeyes robustly, adding to Sloan's great surprise, 'The police aren't perfect, you know, any more than doctors are and it's a great mistake for anyone to think they are . . . Doctors lose patients just as the police lose people, and they don't let it put them off their stride.' He grunted. 'And neither should you. Wouldn't do at all.'

'Thank you, sir.'

'Makes for a lot of trouble, that way of thinking,' said Leeyes, who to Sloan's certain knowledge had never admitted any such thing before. 'Myself, I think there's a lot to be said for faith healing. Now, tell me, where do those two pretty boys at Staple St James come in?'

'Ah . . . I'll tell you, sir. It's a long story.'

After he'd left Dr Chomel on the Saturday afternoon Sloan had been driven back to Staple St James by an indefatigable Crosby. George Gledhill and Mike Itchen were where they'd been when he'd left them. The two scientists might have been cast in stone as the policeman recounted what had become of Dr Byville. The news, though, loosened their tongues.

'He just wouldn't take no for an answer, I suppose,' burst out Gledhill, 'the cold-blooded old devil.'

'He always did think he was cleverer than anyone else,' commented Mike Itchen. 'Mind you, he was really upset when the Hospital Ethics Committee said he couldn't do what he wanted.'

'You'd have thought he would have stopped when half the patients died,' said Gledhill, adding by way of explanation to the two policemen, 'That's our cut-off point with animals, by the way.'

'You better hadn't tell young Darren Clements that,' remarked Crosby. 'He and his little friends might come back.'

'Just for the record,' said Sloan, sticking to the point, 'did whatever Byville was using come from here?'

Both men were adamant that his supplies hadn't come from Gilroy's Pharmaceuticals.

'The Cardigan Protocol, yes,' said Gledhill unhesitatingly. 'Roger Byville's substances, whatever they were, definitely not. It should be quite easy to check, if you wish, Inspector.'

'Thank you, sir.' He coughed. 'There are just one or two other things to be followed up before we go.'

'Of course,' said Gledhill, running a dry tongue over even drier lips. 'Go on.'

'And someone else whom we'd like to see.'

'Who's that?' stammered Gledhill nervously.

'The man whom you'd arranged for Dr Meggie to meet here on Friday,' spelt out Sloan. 'At lunchtime. Remember?'

'Oh, him.' Relief flowed out of Gledhill's voice while Mike Itchen's taut posture immediately slackened. 'That was only Al Dexter of Dexter Palindome over at Luston. He had been getting ready to take a look at the Cardigan Protocol with a view to advising us on any possible production difficulties, that's all.'

'And will there be any difficulties?' enquired Sloan.

'Too soon to say,' returned Gledhill hurriedly. 'Much too soon.'

'But the trial was completed, wasn't it?' said Sloan innocently.

'Yes, yes, Inspector, but we will still need to do a lot of work on it, won't we, Mike?'

'Quite a lot.' Itchen hastened to agree with him.

'Why?' asked Sloan mildly. 'You've told me that you'd already got the meeting with Al – Dexter, I think you said the name was – lined up for just that very purpose.'

'You've still got Dr Meggie's workings, that's why,' said Gledhill, tiny beads of sweat breaking out on his forehead. 'We'd need them before we could get much further.'

'I am sure', said Sloan formally, 'that we shall be able to let you have copies in due course.'

Mike Itchen leaned forward. 'And when might that be, Inspector?'

'After our scientists have been over them,' said Sloan pleasantly. 'I'm sure you'll understand that they'll need to examine them pretty closely first.'

Gledhill's face took on a greyish tinge. 'Thank you, Inspector,' he managed with a visible effort. 'Perhaps then we'll talk to Al Dexter again.'

'We, Crosby,' had declared Sloan once they were back in the privacy of the police car, 'on the other hand are going to talk to Al Dexter now. Get us over to Luston, will you? I don't like loose ends.'

There was something else, too. Talking to Gledhill and Itchen had been too much like playing hunt-the-thimble for Sloan's liking. All it had needed was a room full of excited small children calling out 'Getting warmer' and 'Getting colder'. The message when Al Dexter's name had been mentioned was definitely 'Getting colder': that was when both men had visibly relaxed. It would do no harm at all, Sloan had decided, to talk to Al Dexter of Dexter Palindome (Luston) plc. They tracked him down at his home at the better end of the town.

'Sure, Inspector,' the manufacturer said laconically, 'I'm ready to take on making Cardigan for the wider world just as soon as Gilroy's give the word. They know that.' He cocked an enquiring eyebrow at the two policemen. 'It sounded to me as if they'd developed a really worthwhile product.'

'Good,' said Sloan absently.

'And one without any side-effects.'

'I see,' said Sloan. 'Presumably that's good, too?'

'They're often the problem, you know.' He tapped his finger. 'Side-effects can make or break a product.'

Sloan said that he could see that they might, and that the patients might not like them either.

'And, as I understand it,' drawled Dexter, 'the beauty of Cardigan is that it doesn't have any.'

'Just the one,' said Detective Constable Crosby,

who must have been listening in spite of all appearances to the contrary.

Dexter looked up alertly. 'What's that?'

'All the people on it suddenly lost a lot of weight,' said Crosby, turning to Sloan. 'Don't you remember, sir?'

'So that's what they were up to! Testing Naomite,' exploded Dexter, a man transformed. For one wild moment Sloan thought the drug manufacturer was going to grab Crosby by the throat and shake him. 'Say that again, Constable,' he breathed, 'and then show me the evidence. This, I want to see with my own eyes.'

'Apparently,' said Sloan, valiantly trying now to reduce scientific perfidy to bite-sized pieces for consumption by the superintendent, 'Gledhill and Itchen were working their own little fiddle on the side.'

'Ah, they were, were they?' grunted Leeyes.

'They were riding on the back of Dr Paul Meggie's Cardigan trials – not that he knew, poor fellow.'

'How?'

'They were conducting a little nested case control study all of their own—'

'Sounds to me more like they were lining their own nests,' sniffed Leeyes.

'—of something they had developed called Naomite.' It had been Boaz who had 'bought all at the hand of Naomi' but that had been in the Old Testament and the superintendent wouldn't want to know that.

'Sloan, I am only a policeman, not a Nobel prize-winner.'

'It's like this, sir.' Sloan had had the benefit of a lecture by Al Dexter. That entrepreneur had been very interested indeed in what Gledhill and Itchen had been up to. But not surprised.

Sloan said, 'They set up this neat little scheme of testing something of their own under the umbrella of Dr Meggie's perfectly proper pilot scheme which had been duly approved by all the regulatory authorities.'

'Clever,' nodded Leeyes.

'Very clever,' endorsed Sloan, briefed by Al Dexter, 'because by using the subjects Dr Meggie'd selected they'd found a way of getting more accurately matched controls and reducing some of the variables and so they didn't need as large a study.'

'And I suppose', said Leeyes, waving a hand, 'they'll argue they were doing it all for the good of mankind anyway.'

'Well,' said Sloan cautiously, 'they were looking for the Holy Grail of all research pharmacists—'

'A cure for cancer?'

'An instant treatment for obesity,' said Sloan, coached by the realist from Dexter Palindome

(Luston) plc. 'Without a doubt they'd have been millionaires overnight, the pair of 'em.'

'Where to, sir?' Detective Constable Crosby asked Sloan as he joined him in the car.

'Kinnisport Hospital,' said Sloan. 'To see an artist about his painting.'

'Oh, him,' said Crosby dismissively. 'Full of funny ideas, he is.'

'You've seen Dr Dabbe's report?' The pathologist had returned from his weekend in high good humour, the yachting trophy safely under his arm for another year.

'What about it?' asked Crosby.

'Dr Dabbe says Martin Friar was poisoned with fagarine all right as well as one or two other things.'

'And Dr Byville won't say anything,' said Crosby. 'He's a cool one, isn't he, sir? Just sitting there and asking for his solicitor.'

'You know, Crosby, somehow I don't think that's going to make a lot of difference now.'

Sloan was even more sure about this when they'd spoken to Adrian Gomm. The artist had painted a second alembic on the other side – the left half – of the mural. Where the first one had been coloured green, this one, splashing fluid out of the flask, was red.

'I call it a parable for our time, Inspector,' he said.

'Good drugs on the one hand and bad ones on the other.'

'Quite so,' said Sloan. 'Two sides of the same coin, you might say, sir,' he added, since money came into both sides, too. He knew that now with a vengeance. 'Can you by any chance recollect whether you were up your ladder when Dr Byville left Dr Friar on Saturday morning?'

'Sure.' The artist leaned forward and applied a brush stroke of red paint to the left-hand alembic. 'Dr Friar walked him out to his car. Toadying, I'd have called it if I hadn't heard them talking in the hall first.'

'Go on.'

'They were discussing a spleen patient who'd just died on the ward, and Dr Byville was telling Dr Friar not to let it worry him.' Gomm drew himself up. 'I hope someone would worry if I kicked the bucket that young.'

'The Administrator would if you hadn't finished this first,' said Crosby, adding disparagingly, 'unless he's paying you by the yard.'

'Then what?' said Detective Inspector Sloan sharply. Dr Meggie's murder by Roger Byville would be more difficult to prove than Dr Friar's and what he wanted was more evidence than carbon monoxide poisoning by someone with access to helium and a riot-control agent.

'Dr Byville told him to come to his car with him

and he'd give him a swig of something to make him feel better,' said the artist, rubbing grubby fingers down a grubby shirt.

'A Mickey Finn,' nodded Crosby.

Sloan leaned forward. 'You could see into the car park through that high window, couldn't you?' he said persuasively, 'because you saw those boys playing round our car when we were here.'

'Oh, yes,' said Gomm, unaware that he had at that moment stopped being merely a commentator on good and evil in society and had become, willy-nilly, a player in the game of life. 'Dr Byville got a flask out of his car and handed it to Dr Friar. He took a swig. I saw him.'

Detective Constable Crosby turned the car back towards Berebury, automatically overtaking some traffic he considered dilatory. 'Clever of Byville to use some of the stuff from the Cardigan Protocol to kill Dr Friar with, wasn't it?'

'Fagarine,' mused Sloan. 'Dr Dabbe seemed to think it might have a future as a useful drug for the heart.'

'So that only leaves the paperwork then, doesn't it, sir?'

'Yes. And that means', Sloan prompted him gently, 'that there's no hurry any more and therefore you needn't drive so fast, Crosby. Cardigan's over now.'

'Yes, sir.' He steered the car smartly past a couple

of traffic-calming measures at speed and said confidentially, 'You know, sir, I worked out why it was called Cardigan.'

'Did you?'

'Because "cardiac" means "appertaining to the heart". I asked Dr Dabbe. Clever, isn't it?'